THE LESS THAN PERFECT LEGEND OF
DONNA CREOSOTE

THE
LESS THAN
PERFECT
LEGEND
OF DONNA
CREOSOTE

by Dan Micklethwaite

Bluemoose

First published in 2016 by
Bluemoose Books Ltd
25 Sackville Street
Hebden Bridge
West Yorkshire
HX7 7DJ

www.bluemoosebooks.com

British Library Cataloguing-in-Publication data
A catalogue record for this book is available from the British Library

Hardback ISBN 978-1-910422-17-5

Paperback ISBN 978-1-910422-18-2

Printed and bound in the UK by Short Run Press

For my parents

1

Nobody had ever accused Donna Crick-Oakley of being adventurous.

A slut, yes. A thickie. A dreamer. A quiet one. A fat bitch (before she lost weight). A skinny bitch (after). A nutter. A swot. A stick-in-the-mud. An accident waiting to happen. A cry-baby. A silly cow. A giant waste of time.

All of the above, but never adventurous.

The fact was, when given a choice between real life and books, Donna Crick-Oakley chose books every time.

Of course, she hadn't sprung forth from the womb being able to read, and had never devoted the entirety of her days to the practice. It was more the case that when real life disappointed her she selected certain stories as her preferred location of retreat.

The other kids hadn't liked that she always seemed to get more fun from paper than she ever did from them. And other adults didn't seem to like it, either.

At least, Kirk hadn't seemed to.

But she kept on choosing books.

She chose books because they never left her lonely the way that Kirk had left her lonely. Because company was often nothing of the kind, whereas a good book always was.

She chose books for the smell of fresh-pressed pages, or for the yellow-brown musk of library mould, but always for the breathy kiss of paper rustling. She chose books because some of them held prose that made her weep, or poetry that winded her, and words that made her heart skip beats.

She chose books because some came ready-made with characters that seemed like perfect versions of herself, all of them little proofs that somehow, somewhere, it might just be possible for her to be better: to be popular, powerful, sexy and smart.

She chose books because they lied to her with more conviction than real people ever had.

Her flat, in a tower block, was full of them.
Three thousand, four hundred and seventy-two of them.
Mostly fairy tale, fantasy, medieval romance and myth.

There were three rooms – an open-plan kitchen-cum-lounge, a bedroom, and a bathroom – and she kept at least two tall bookcases in each. Even in the bathroom, much to the surprise and amusement of her occasional guests.

To stop the books getting damp, she'd fixed shower curtains to the front of the bookcase by the toilet and the one by the sink. She'd hoped to find transparent ones but had settled instead for an opaque beige, so whenever she reached behind them she was never quite sure which book she'd get.

She'd read most of them before, of course, but she still enjoyed surprises.

So long as the surprises didn't involve an ambush set by bandits, Vikings, highwaymen or dragons.

In her bedroom, the bookcases and wardrobe that covered the walls were packed solid, and she'd resorted to storing her surplus in less regular ways.

At painstaking length and effort, she had gathered all the works in her collection that were the same depth: roughly three-fifty pages, from front cover to back. And then she'd covered the floor with a kind of erudite rug.

She may have been at the highest level of the tower block but, in here at least, she had the lowest ceiling.

When Kirk had first visited, he'd scoffed at this system, dedicating whole minutes of the evening to asking why she had so many books, why she had books in the bathroom, why she had books like a big cardboardy carpet spread out across her bedroom floor.

The sex, when it came, wasn't impressive.

As a single girl, she didn't spend her time on social networking or dating sites searching for her next potential beau.

She didn't cycle through her Friends list, studying the profile of each boy on there – the ones with whom she hadn't already had some kind of encounter – wondering if they were likewise lonely, if they'd be up for a bit of fun. And, if so, what they'd be like, and if they too would refuse to remove their socks on account of book covers being sticky.

Not any more.

She certainly didn't stand on her balcony, staring down across the rooftops of Huddersfield, telling herself: *My prince is out there. Somewhere.* Before bursting into song.

Not then.

She just read.

It was her father, an English teacher, who started her with that.

Ever since she could remember, he had come home from school ranting about the rising rate of illiteracy, and about how kids these days were, mostly, stupid fuckers. Every night since she could remember, her mother had reprimanded him for using foul language, they'd argued for half an hour, on average, and

3

the fights had generally concluded with her father vowing: *No daughter of mine is going to grow up like that: as a... a thickie!*

After that, almost every night she could remember, he had come into her room and ordered her to read something to him, for another half an hour.

This, he claimed, had the dual benefit of helping her intellectually, and calming him down enough that he could stomach *whatever slop your mother's going to put on the table tonight.*

There had been a few breaks in this practice, of course, a litany of small defections: to geography, for about a week; to history; to an after-school hockey club, on and off for several years. A few times, she had even thrown herself wholeheartedly into mathematics, discovering an unexpected aptitude for figures. An affinity for algebra, once she got to that level.

But something in the turn of textbook pages always brought her back.

And so, rather than redoubling her efforts and vowing to rid herself of everything to do with such stories as soon as she was able, Donna Crick-Oakley simply climbed further in. She had found in them the most effective evasion, the most delightful deliverance from the turmoil that was, until her parents' inevitable divorce, her family home.

Two months after that divorce, and five years before today, her father had decided that she, just like her mother, was a giant waste of time, and that he had no interest in seeing either of them any longer. He'd moved away. Down south at first, and then out of the country.

Before he left, however, he had been mandated by the court to pay them both a sum in lieu of maintenance. He was given the option to either pay the sum in advance, or deposit it in monthly instalments.

He chose the former option. Another kind of surprise that Donna didn't like.

Despite her mother's vicious and repeated questioning of how he'd managed to keep such an amount squirrelled away, no explanation was ever provided.

He just stayed quiet, expressionless, and signed the court papers.

Left a six-figure phantom in place of a husband and dad.

Two weeks later, as an acknowledgement of some lingering paternal bond, or debt, he sent her a letter, along with the sizeable cheque:

> *Dear Donna,*
>
> *If you still want to take your daddy's advice, I would suggest using this to get the hell out of Huddersfield and never looking back. There's nothing even close to good enough there for a daughter of mine.*
>
> *What's left of my love,*
>
> *Charles Oakley*
>
> *x*

But she used the money instead to make a life out of books.

2

Nobody believed Donna Crick-Oakley when she told them she didn't much care for Disney films.

How could she not?

They were full of fairy stories.

Weren't fairy stories her thing?

Her failure to like them wasn't absolute.

She enjoyed the beginnings of the earlier ones. The first minute or so, when the camera focused in on a tenderly-rendered image of a leather-bound tome; when the cover opened, independently, the magic behind the motion subtly implied. When the camera found those four small yet special words: *Once upon a time...*

Where Disney films fell down, for her – in fact, where most films fell down – lay in their decision to abandon that string of words thereafter. Through their insistence on providing pictorial representations of things that she would prefer to imagine, they lost her interest, offended her, even, on some level.

She did not, when she read of a prince – charming or otherwise – think of him as having dark hair and no lines on his face. She did not think of him as having hair that was flaxen or brown or grey, or purple either, but that wasn't really the point.

Books allowed for the possibility that her idea of Prince Charming might change.

Disney films didn't.

Whenever she found herself watching them, usually with a new man, she tended to drift off, to move away from the plot and the action into wondering if the cartoon Cinderella really did fall for her Prince Charming the first time they met. If the dream bloke the would-be princess had built up in her head was in fact completely different from the one that she'd found. Or who had found her.

If, when she'd first learnt to touch herself, she'd had another face in mind.

As regards her own situation with Kirk, that had certainly been the case.

As it had with the other four men she'd slept with, for that matter.

She didn't think Kirk was likely to be anyone's idea of a prince, charming or otherwise. He had blue eyes, but he hid them behind bright and shiny red and black glasses. He was well-built, especially his upper-body, but he covered his potentially appealing attributes with crumpled, age-inappropriate T-shirts, and also with backne.

He didn't have dark hair, at least, but then he also didn't wash it.

This resulted in what her mother would call a hodgepodge, which looked to Donna like a mix between dreadlocks and dead hamsters. A state regrettably replicated at his less-than-spectacular crotch.

And *he* had criticised *her* apartment.

To calm herself, to pull herself back from the edge of such thoughts, she liked, before going to bed, to take off her socks and press her toes against the book covers.

They weren't sticky at all.

They felt expensive, like marble tiles, the kind they might have in the foyers of five-star hotels, perched on the edge of bright azure oceans.

Or in the entrance halls of castles. The kind that slightly mad Bavarians once built on top of grimly timbered Alps.

3

Nobody now seemed to see eye-to-eye with Donna Crick-Oakley on the issues that mattered to her most.

Her mum didn't, anyway.

The few occasions that Donna actually sanctioned a visit, she was told it was time she grew up and got rid.

Books in the bathroom? Really? They'll get damp. They'll go mouldy, and who'll take them off your hands then? Not charity shops, that's for sure. They can't make money for starving homeless refugee children with water-damaged goods. Rotting copies of Narnia aren't going to put rice on anybody's plate.

And as for your bedroom...

Was this why so many books wound up in charity shops? Donna wondered.

For the sake of a little more space?

Some nights, even after the calm of her feet on the marble, that question weighed so heavy that she couldn't get to sleep.

Why didn't people seem to want books beside them at all times, just in case?

Just in case they were too alone. Just in case they were ill and watching TV would make too many too-loud noises. Just in case they'd had a shitty day at school or at work, or at the weekend, when by rights their problems should have had the decency to cut them some slack and leave them alone. Just in case they got stood up by a dickhead with spots on his back and no fashion sense. Just in case some bitch broke their heart. Just in case they wanted to open a bottle of wine, but needed somebody to share it with. Just in case they remembered a line, out of the blue, and felt the urgent want to rummage through shelf after shelf until they found where it lived. Just in case they wanted to keep reading after they'd searched out that sentence.

Just in case they needed something in their life that they could turn to in times of stagnation, for ideas, and for answers, and for hope.

4

Nobody, least of all Donna Crick-Oakley, expected that she would turn to books for ideas in quite such a way.

In the mornings, rather than taking the time to reacquaint her feet with the literary lino she'd installed, she was generally eager to get up and wash.

Such had been her need for bookcase space that she'd set one up in front of the window, meaning that even when it wasn't too warm outside – which, this being West Yorkshire, was more often than not – it was still fairly close to baking in her room. Though the temperature dropped during the night, she would quite often wake feeling clammy with sweat.

This morning, she took her shower as usual. She scrubbed herself thoroughly but quickly with a loofah, not paying too much attention to her body as she did so.

Then, having dried herself, she eased onto the clean wooden horseshoe of the toilet seat, and fumbled behind the shower curtain that covered the bookcase to her left.

She withdrew a hefty second-hand volume which she knew, having already read it seven times, involved witches, dragons, knights – one braver, bolder and generally better than all others – kings, counts, princesses – one more pretty, more perfect and more predisposed to getting herself in distress than all others – stallions, wolves, woodcutters, and a not-particularly-witty talking toad.

The buying of second-hand books was, for Donna, somewhat akin to pet rescue. Had this volume been a dog, it might have been bloated and balding and missing some teeth.

Yet such was her compassion for afflicted creatures that, upon noticing the book there on the charity shop shelf, its raggedy spine bandaged to its body with peeling strips of parcel tape, she'd been unable to leave the premises without it.

She had brought only a small handbag, so the poor mangy thing was left poking out of the top, its spine lolling like a tongue to make the most of fresh air.

Now it sat coddled upon the softness of her palms.

The miracle of such stories, to Donna, was that they could be opened to pretty much any page and the essence of what was visible would be more or less the same. There was always some manner of evil, doing that lurking thing it does. There was always somebody in need of saving from that evil. There was always somebody – or a queue of somebodies – ready to save that poor, imperilled soul.

There was always questing to be done, in short, to have a chance to set things right.

And Donna liked it when that happened.

She used to know quite a few people who'd liked that as well, but gone about it differently.

Some had spent most of their money on amassing stacks of discs for console play. They'd spend hours upon their parents' sofas, slashing at demons or pumping blue plasma streams into alien hordes.

Others had saved their pennies to subscribe to online roleplaying games. Games that offered not only the option to create an avatar from scratch, but of choosing whether that character would be good, or whether they'd get busy lurking. You could step inside and sway the story, they'd told her. You could go beyond the story and fill in all of the free-roaming gaps. You could wander the land on your own, if you wanted to, and not do much of anything. Or you could go down to market with the rest of your guild.

If you spent enough hours in that game-world, they'd said, it was pretty much like real life.

Only better, because you could do really cool things like go hunting orcs, and then trade orc hides for gold, and then use that gold to buy bigger swords to go hunting trolls with.

At the behest of a boyfriend two before Kirk, she had given these online RPGs a shot.

Make your own avatar, he'd said, *have a go at the training. See if you can get the hang of all the controls.* It was keyboard and mouse only.

Twenty minutes became two hours, became five or six hours, daily. Between that and the books she still read, she barely had any time left for him. Not outside of the game. Then they began to grow distant inside it as well. After he caught her Sorceress-class character flirting in text-speak with a Ranger, he called her a slut and said he hoped she got herpes. Then he shut down his laptop, downed his cola and left.

He phoned her a few days later to apologise, to say he sincerely hoped she never, ever, ever got herpes, or gonorrhoea, or any other STI, and that he honestly didn't think she was the kind of girl who would. He said he hoped as well that she forgave him and still wanted to see him again. Even if they were only really good friends and never did it again or anything like that.

But maybe they could still snog, or just cuddle up in front of a film on the sofa?

No. The damage had been done. She deleted her game account. She deleted his number. She blocked him on her social network page, and stopped checking her newsfeed so often after that.

It was pretty much like real life, they'd told her.
And that was the problem.

Donna didn't see the point in her escape becoming more like what she was escaping. If anything, she thought, real life could stand to be much more like her books.
Perhaps then she'd actually be inclined to go out and take part.

With that in mind – always at the back of her mind but especially brightly and sharply this morning – she looked down at the story, the words on the page. Maybe eight times was too many to read the same thing, no matter how great its pleasures, or to try hiding away in the same old spot.

Maybe it was time she stopped hiding entirely.

Maybe, she thought, as she stood up from the toilet, it was time she went out and tried changing the world.

5

Nobody had ever accused Donna Crick-Oakley of being adventurous, but adventurous was what she very much intended to become.

Of course, she couldn't just go out adventuring dressed as she was.

Not least because, well, she wasn't.

There was a full-length mirror on her wardrobe door, the only space that she could find for it to fit. Forgetting her purpose for a moment, she started searching with harsh eyes for the parts of her that must have displeased Kirk and the four men before him. And the countless others who'd decided against.

She didn't have to search long.

She unwound the towel from around her hair, let it unravel and frame her cheeks.

She called it red. Strawberry blonde. Auburn.

They, the other kids, had called it *ginger*.

Ginger was a spice. Was a Spice Girl, if it came to that. It was something that you put in biscuits, or in tea, or in curries, or on terrible, and terribly catchy, hit singles in the late 1990's. It wasn't her.

But that wasn't her choice.

She'd got the feeling that perhaps it was something that her boyfriends tolerated, rather than desired, and none of them had ever really outright praised it; a couple of them, Kirk, surprisingly, not included, had made *well-meaning* jokes about it from time to time.

Beneath the fraying ends, her collarbone was too noticeable. The result of being thin, of being lanky. Now.

And the result of an accident she'd had when she was seven-and-three-quarter years old. Falling off her bike. Tumbling over the handlebars and into the tarmac, which, as ever, failed to forgive.

There had been crying, and her tears had done magic and united her parents. Or reunited them. Maybe. Her father had been especially joyful, because her injury and subsequent trip to the hospital had necessitated his leaving school early, ducking out on a training day. Cutting class, he'd called it – one of the few times she could remember him showing a kind of throwback teenage glee.

He'd still brought a book with him, though. He'd already had it in the car. He pulled it out of a shopping bag like a white rabbit, like a tarot card announcing an unavoidable fate. Donna had read it, whispered it, in the waiting room, though she couldn't recall now which book it had been. Only remembered sitting at the edge of a rough plastic chair, gritting her teeth, willing a nurse, any nurse, to call out her name.

To say to her: It's Ok. The doctor will see you now.

When she'd been fat, in her early teens, her breasts had been larger. It was a shame that everything else about her had been larger as well, and so any benefits those C-cups might have given her were rendered moot and insubstantial.

Now, depending on the man, and on how much she'd recently been eating, they struggled to register as even a good handful.

The boyfriend before Kirk hadn't seemed to mind, had told her he thought they were wonderful, perky. He had spent enough time toying with the nipples, drawing a fingertip round them in spirograph circles, his own erection noticeably heightened when those nipples were at their longest and hardest and he reached out with his tongue.

But Kirk hadn't given them much consideration at all.

At the sides of what she still referred to as her tummy, just above her hips, there were stretchmarks. Sometimes she thought they looked like dragon-scratches, as though she'd been ambushed. The bad kind of surprise.

She had long wanted to wake up to a good surprise, to catch a glimpse of those spaces around her hips and find the stretchmarks flattened, gone.

She had long been frustrated.

Those hips themselves were problematic.

Again, back when she'd been a bigger girl, they'd been fuller, and, she had thought, seemed more viably fecund. She had looked at herself in mirrors then, and, along with the paunch of puppy fat she carried, it had been easy to imagine herself as a soon-to-be mother.

Now, her hips were bony and angular, and were not, Donna thought, of the kind that anyone would look at and label 'child-bearing'.

Her knickers were the site of the most striking and the most secret of her hypocrisies.

She owned hardly any that weren't emblazoned with the face of some cartoon character or other.

When this had been pointed out to her, and she had been forced to defend yet again her stance as regards Disney, she'd protested that on underwear those cartoons didn't explicitly form part of a story. They weren't trying to influence her perception of a classic character type as located within a classic story structure. They were simply cool, cute drawings.

This argument had not been bought, entirely, by either of the parties involved.

As she thought about it now, it seemed to Donna that she chose underwear like this because she had difficulty seeing herself as sexy, and couldn't seriously consider purchasing some fancy lace knickers from one of those lingerie stores.

And yet, she remained aware that she had difficulty seeing herself as sexy because she didn't wear fancy lace knickers.

Beside today's cartoon face, there were small curls of ginger hair. Auburn hair. Red. Doubling back on themselves, reaching up and around the elastic at the top of her thighs.

In the mirror, Belle looked back all bearded. Beastly.

Donna was aware too that most men nowadays didn't seem to find that attractive, but she had not had time, nor reason, to trim or shave or wax, of late. Either there or on her legs.

She took small comfort in knowing that Kirk hadn't been in any position to complain.

The purple and silver polish on her toenails was cracked and peeling. It looked as though she'd stubbed her toes and the bruises hadn't cleared.

Even without those blemishes, her feet were nobody's prize. They were thin – like the rest of her, now – and long. Slightly longer than her forearm, in fact, and so whenever she looked too closely at them she felt a little like a freak.

She always shut her eyes when she had those feet naked on top of her books at bedtime.

That allowed her to visualise the castle better, too.
Sometimes.

Sometimes, in the entrance hall, she could even see the chandelier.

6

Donna Crick-Oakley had never been clothes-shopping with anyone apart from her mother – who had never, by Donna's reckoning, done a capable job.

Her mother was colour-blind, but stubborn in her refusal to admit it. She also had a fondness for shoulder pads and frills.

As a consequence, the contents of Donna's wardrobe didn't really suit her plan.

After all, one could not wear a blue-and-white-striped boob-tube and expect to be taken seriously as a knight errant.

Ditto for plaid mini-skirts.

Double-ditto for jeggings that had worn down at the knees.

Indeed, she reflected, it might well have been better to approach this from the opposite direction: to rummage through the dressing-up box first and then adapt her choice of character accordingly.

But Donna didn't want to do that.

She was set on being a knight.

Not simply because, from a lot of the books she'd read, she knew that a great deal of the finest and most fantastic quests began with their involvement. But also because, if she was going make this change in Huddersfield, she'd prefer to be in armour.

Of course, these days, the traditional suit of armour could be – and often was – swapped for any number of other uniforms, but Donna had always been a sucker for the classic styling. There was just something about the chainmail, the curved and detailed metal of the breastplate and the helmet, which struck her as incontrovertibly heroic.

Mystical, too.

Anachronistic.

Anarchic, even.

The first time she'd actually seen some, in the flesh, moving around rather than just behind glass, her little mind went so far as to suspect some kind of witchcraft. She was eight, and her dad had taken her to see a jousting tournament at the Royal Armouries in Leeds. The contestants, as they rode into the ring, hadn't quite seemed to belong to the same world as the crowd: as though they'd burst out of history and back into life. Or, maybe more likely, had dragged the crowd with them to some place in between.

They were outliers, renegades, the unusual suspects.

And they were all the more appealing, to Donna, for that.

She had never really fit in anywhere either.

And yet they gave her hope of being cool just the same.

However, the closest things she could find were an old pair of work trousers, a shade lighter than charcoal, that had only seen service twice, and a grey hoody that she wore, by her mother's tally, far too often.

Not exactly a combination to inspire epic poems.

For starters, neither of them was anywhere near shiny enough.

Wearing the work pants – which, unfortunately, she had no time to iron – she bore the hoody to the kitchen like a folded-up flag, like a prize to present to the tournament victor. She spread it out on the table.

There were no slogans or logos on its front for her to cover, nor on the back. Nevertheless, she did think that it could do with more in the way of armour-plating. The colour grey's close proximity to steel, and the thickness of the fabric, would not in themselves prove sufficient protection.

Should the massed hordes of her hometown rise up in pursuit.

Perhaps a baking tray, then.

Or two.

And another.

And some aluminium foil, possibly, to provide that much-needed shine.

Donna Crick-Oakley always kept well-stocked with duct tape, not only to keep the more mangy of her novels together, but also to help shore up deficiencies in her bookcase shelves. She used it now to fix a baking tray breadthways across the chest area of the hoody, and a small pizza tray covering the lower torso. She stuck a larger baking tray lengthways to cover the spine.

She taped the aluminium foil around the sleeves, trying not to pinch the fabric too tightly. She applied the same sheathing technique to her charcoal-grey trousers, trying not to tourniquet herself in the process and thereby stop the circulation to her hairy legs and freaky feet.

And what about hiding those feet?

She had a pair of silver, sequinned flats somewhere – possibly buried at the bottom of her wardrobe – but she wasn't sure they'd really go. They were probably too dainty for the kind of derring-do that might occur.

Somewhere else, there was a pair of old Doc Martens but they, to be honest, were a little too... purple. She could always cover them with foil or duct tape as well, of course, but she wasn't sure what that would do to the leather.

Still, she supposed that wouldn't matter, if everything went as she hoped.

It was only when she was trying these out, standing in front of the mirror, that she realised that she was going to need something to cover her head, to complete the ensemble.

Probably the most helmet-like items she possessed were the three pans – small, medium and large, in proper Goldilocks fashion – that hung on a rack she'd fixed over the hob.

She pulled up her hood before she tried them for size.

The medium one fit best. Just right, in fact.

In order to avoid any awkwardness, however, and to avoid being party to the accidental blinding of any tall folks out in town, she opted to unscrew and set aside the handle.

Yet she felt there was still something missing.

A visor.

All the best helmets should have one of those.

A colander would be too large and unwieldy, that much was obvious. Not to mention just a little too daft. Besides, it seemed more Civil War and not quite chivalric. Of all the other things in her kitchen that might provide the necessary amount of both protection and mystery, only two seemed vaguely viable: a slotted metal fish-slice and a large, flat cheese-grater.

The latter, by the looks of it, had more surface-area, and so it was that which she duct-taped in front of her face.

With her bare hands. Which wouldn't do.

She used the last of the tape to wrap what was left of the foil around her palms, across her knuckles, the way a boxer might beneath their gloves. That was all she could think of for gauntlets, as she didn't have any suitable gloves of her own.

Except for some almost wire-wool-looking ones that she'd bought as part of an exfoliation regime which hadn't yet, if she was honest, really got going. They were a bit itchy, and seemed to take more skin off her fingers than anywhere else.

Standing in front of the mirror for the third time, peering at herself through the holes in her makeshift visor, she was half proud and yet still half disappointed. It was certainly a good effort, she felt, for the hour or so it had taken. And she more or less looked the part.

But it wasn't quite up to the Royal Armouries' standard.

Still, she guessed those performers had a blacksmith they could call on, or some other skilled metal-worker. And such smiths, as far as Donna was aware, did not, even nowadays, have to work where they cooked.

The only other alternative, as far as Donna could see, was to pay a visit to her mother. To ask politely to borrow her sewing machine and a selection of the sparkly cloth that she kept bundled in boxes under the stairs. A monstrous commingling of outgrown boleros; an archive of spandex and rayon and sateen.

She went with the grey hoody and the aluminium and the baking tray and the pan without its handle and the cheese-grater fitted as a visor to the front.

Which she felt made her look just about knightly enough.

7

Usually, if Donna Crick-Oakley left her flat, she did so at times when nobody else was likely to be leaving theirs.

Today, setting out at half-past ten, too late for work but too early for lunch, she anticipated being in the lift on her own, surrounded by the still-surprisingly-shiny, graffiti-free walls and, in those surroundings, looking perfectly at home.

She was to be frustrated.

Two floors down, out of twelve, the lift came to a halt. The doors parted, grindingly as ever, and there stood a woman, maybe her own age, with a child in a pram.

Donna had never seen this other woman before and so she assumed that the other woman had, in turn, never seen her. They had certainly never been introduced, nor held a conversation. Not even small talk.

Donna was struggling to see her now, in truth, with the cheese grater in the way, but the few features she could make out did not look particularly impressed. It wasn't an ideal way to meet a neighbour, she had to admit.

Respectfully and carefully, she took off her helmet and stepped back against the wall, offering the woman more space in the lift. The foil of her gauntlets crackled as she did so.

The child started crying.

The woman made no attempt to quiet her offspring, but simply stared at Donna. Head cocked to the side and a sly *What the fuck?* on the tip of her tongue, albeit never quite making it out.

The woman was wearing bright cyan joggers with four stripes down each side, and a lime green tee that didn't quite cover her midriff; she had a clutch of black-inked hearts and stars tattooed like a status update on her inside left wrist.

What the fuck? indeed, Donna thought.

When the lift reached the ground floor, the woman wheeled her still-wailing child to the exit. On her way, Donna thought she heard the woman start to mutter something but, with her hood still covering her ears, she couldn't be sure.

She waited for the woman to leave before putting the helmet back on and following her out through the door.

The woman turned right and Donna turned left.

The brand new knight errant felt her boldness returning.

She would need it, she thought.

There was a big road to cross.

Traffic looked even more cram-jammed down here than it usually did from her balcony, but in spite of its density it was still flowing fast. There would be no way to pass from this side to the other without using the traffic lights, a good fifty metres ahead.

The distance seemed to stretch, seemed hazardous on its own, fragmented as it was through the visor, and all the cars speeding past her set her on edge. She knew she had to do something to keep her mind steady.

Rattling forwards, she told herself: I'm a knight, I'm a knight, and she began to think about her progress in much more medieval terms. Not vocabulary-wise, for Chaucer did not rank among her favourite authors, but rather she envisioned her surroundings as they might have been back then.

On the other side of the road, she could make out a betting shop.

Inside, fat men in felt jerkins jangled pouches of gold.

Skinny men sagged out through the oak door in defeat.

A few buildings down, an estate agent's crowded window.

Scraps of vellum and bark showcased various hovels, available on a 'buy to let the peasants work' basis, ranging from your basic wattle and daub to your fancier, sturdier timber and thatch.

Cosy enough, Donna guessed, but no towers, no keep.

And next to her now, on this side of the road, the revolving door of the Jobcentre Plus.

Which it wasn't too much of a stretch to squint at and think: Dungeon.

She did, after all, recall its cells well.

She'd done a stretch there for a while, after she moved out but before her dad left entirely. That was how she'd landed in the temp job for which she'd had to buy these trousers. Which she'd stuck at all of two weeks, until his payment had come through.

Her mother kept mithering her to go back and sign on.

That money won't last you forever, she said.

You need more experience on your sodding CV.

It'll get you out of the house and meeting new people.

But Donna wasn't bothered about meeting new people.

And she had experience to spare that she'd gleaned from her books.

Besides, surely this counted as being out of the house?

Stopped still and so close to it, the road growled even louder; it rushed and harangued, and she was at the edge of

26

a river in a state of near-flood. This crossing became a dock for a rickety ferry and, as she waited for that ferry, in search of further distraction, the pedestrian lights became characters from a morality play.

The red man a devil.

The green man an angel.

Between them, they offered the pilgrim two distinct choices. One good and one bad.

There was no amber for pilgrims, and yet Donna felt very much like she was caught in between.

Because, watching those two figures, the binary outcome they offered, she realised that she had not planned this at all well, beyond her destination, the town centre. The timing of everything, the progression from one part to the next, began to seem arbitrary. Lacking in beauty. Lacking in craft.

In removing the character, the concept of the knight errant, from the pages of her books, she had also separated that concept from the very things she found most appealing about it.

The certainty of enjoyable questing.

The certainty of the hero's success.

It felt too much like a choose-your-own adventure, now – a cop-out from an author who didn't have enough faith in the story they wanted to tell.

Her heavy boots sank down towards vole burrows, squelched amongst the reeds as she shifted her weight.

Dragonflies shivered.

Beyond them, and the midges, and the froth and roil of the water, she studied the lights. They weren't one of those sets that made a noise when it was safe to cross: the ferryman was a mute, or else simply wasn't the talkative type. Rather, you had to watch out for his wave, the slightest of gestures; you had to wait and see which of the men was aglow.

Which, with this visor, was proving a problem.

And – the cheese-grater's handle having got in the way – she hadn't managed to rig up the duct tape as a hinge.

Donna Crick-Oakley removed her helmet again, and held it firmly in the crook of her arm. She imagined it heavy, her head still within. A ghost-story tableau at the side of the road. Or, maybe more suitably, Gawain and the Green Knight.

Only, she wasn't green. And neither yet was the signal.

More's the pity.

Ten cars hurtled by in the space of twenty seconds, and four of them gave a long beep that Dopplered away as they passed. She thought the last one of them had shouted something as well, but she didn't hear what.

She wasn't sure that she wanted to.

Still, as her father had been fond of saying before he left the country and cut all ties: *Nobody ever achieved anything by giving up and going home.*

What had *he* achieved since? Donna wondered.

And pressed on.

When the angel lit up, she took its advice and boarded the ferry. On her way, she endured the sound of five or six more car horns, stretching back along the queue. Not one of them keeping rhythm and time with the next.

She told herself they were swans, or maybe swan-maidens. Jealous of her daring and her long fiery hair.

On the opposite bank, she found herself confronted with an Oriental Supermarket – an apothecary, maybe? – and beside it a building that had been vacant for so long that she couldn't remember its previous use. There wasn't even a sign in the window, or any whitewashed graffiti announcing what it was going to become.

There was only darkness inside now, and she felt drawn, strangely, closer.

It was like the mouth of a monster, or just the cave where it lived.

She stared into it, through her reflection, and told herself she looked fearless. At least, she did when she'd put her helmet back on. She held the pose for a moment, drawing air through her visor. Her chin and her nose were already damp from her breath, but she did her best to ignore it, to ignore everything else.

It was in that state of focus that she noticed something shocking. Something she was more than mildly mortified to admit, even to herself.

She did not have a sword.

Had no weapon of any kind, in fact.

And she was hardly trained in hand-to-hand combat, or any of the martial arts.

After all the hours she'd spent reading of such adventures, she had omitted, in her admittedly rushed preparations, perhaps the most essential element of those heroic tales: the blade with which the dragon or the ogre would be slain.

Even the jousters at the Royal Armouries had lances, and they were just *playing*.

The less said about a shield or a coat of arms, the better.

Under cover of the cheese grater, the knight errant blushed.

8

There were always setbacks in these stories, Donna was well aware of that. Always roadblocks *en route* to the eventual triumph. Always a healthy glimmer of doubt.

It was good for the tension.

Evil wouldn't even *start* lurking if it didn't have a hope in hell of coming out on top.

And there'd be no point in knights questing, if that was the case.

And yet, here she was.

Still bold and still brave.

At the bottom of Beast Market, a shortcut she preferred to the main route uphill.

The name evoked a menagerie of mythical creatures. The patrons outside the street's only pub looked a bit shifty, too, though there were fewer forked tongues at their table and less hybrid anatomy.

That was something to be thankful for, she supposed.

Which was less than could be said for the brewery mascot perched on the roof. An oversized gargoyle, drunk on the job. Always a chance he might lose his balance and fall.

But health and safety regulations were hardly a knight errant's remit.

And the patrons were giving her a few funny looks.

She felt sure there'd be more pressing problems to deal with elsewhere.

Up ahead was the park and beside it the church. At the top of the steeple was the flag of St George, the world-famous dragon-slayer and a true inspiration.

And though she couldn't quite see its full shape through the holes in her mask, the building itself gave a kind of support. Lent her plans weight. This was the first, and maybe the only, example of architecture that she wouldn't have to change.

Certainly, the archway that led through to the steps at the side seemed sublimely medieval.

Not so much the few teens who'd settled on those steps. They were more Neolithic.

One of them stared at her from under a hood that gave the impression of a heavyset brow. He looked as though he was going to stand. Her hands tensed into fists, quite involuntarily. The foil on them crackled.

It was probably best if she didn't pick a fight in holy quarters, though. Right of sanctuary and all that.

She crossed over, hurried along a street lined with takeaways and bars. Bustled past fellow pedestrians with her back held straight and her head held high. Even though the weight of the pan was beginning to tell.

As she reached the Kingsgate Shopping Centre, however, she faltered. It was heaving. Despite it being a weekday there were swarms of people passing both ways through the doors, or loitering around the pillars that underpinned the glassy frontage.

And some of them were beginning to stop and stare.

All in all, she decided, it wasn't perhaps the best place to start searching for work. There would be security staff there already, and they were probably doing a decent job.

She'd leave them to it.

She darted into an arcade thoroughfare, out of the main flow, sunlight leaking in through the roof panels as through a prison cell grating.

She could tell people were following her, albeit discreetly.

She could feel her face getting redder and redder.

Still, she kept her eyes front, in military fashion, and whispered over and over: I'm a knight, I'm a knight. And the clattering of her armour and the crinkling of the foil seemed to beat to that rhythm. The rush of her blood.

More than that, though, more than knightly, Donna felt like a gladiator on the arena approach.

She was still brave and still bold.

She just had to stop dallying.

She had to keep going.

She took a deep breath.

9

P igeons scamper at the sight of her as she strides into the
square.

That group is still following her, but she thinks of them now
as an entourage, a band of supporters, ready to roar her to feats
of great derring-do.

And all of these others, outside a café?
They're just spectators, wanting to see dragons slain.

Nowt wrong wi' that.

In the heart of this plaza, just ahead, is the Library: it's one
of the only spots in town that can outdo her collection, and this
helps maintain her steely resolve. Well, more aluminium. She
is close to the source, she feels, the home of adventure, in the
shadow of a mighty cathedral of words.

If she can't be a knight here, if she can't find the trail of
some great epic narrative, then, in all fairness, what chance has
she got?

Looking out at the crowd, their faces fragmented and
cropped through her visor, she tries to imagine herself even
taller than she seemed in her bedroom – even bigger than she
appeared in that empty shop window – and to be shining like
some magnificent, alien diamond, cut loose from a comet in
centuries past.

She must be that kind of toughness, mustn't she, to have ventured out unarmed?

Indeed, even though she's unarmed – and without a coat *of* arms, even – she imagines that these fair townsfolk will take her for a definitive specimen of boldness and dash, arrived at last to preserve their precious streets as urban idylls. To succeed in that regard where, to look at some of them, other would-be champions have obviously failed.

At least, she wants to.

Those people, though. They're all staring at her, and at each other, a not-so-sly *what the fuck* doing the rounds in between.

Is this some kind of art thing?
You know, put together by one of those ... students.

Or is it, like, a living statue?
But, if so, will it make use of that pan for collecting the change?

And why is it moving?

Is it just some kind of nutter?

Should we call the police?

Is this, Donna wonders, perhaps the horde she predicted?
They do, after all, look a little bit ... rough.

But if she is the knight then that means they are the peasantry, and so, she supposes, that only makes sense. She must make allowances.

She straightens her back again. Holds her head high.
Crunches the foil as she tightens her hands into fists.
Coughs. Clears her throat.

Good people of erm, Huddersfield, I'm here to erm... I'm a brave—

But she can't say anymore. They're beginning to laugh.

It's a young boy who starts it, but it spreads round the group quickly.

They reach for their smartphones, and it feels like torches have been lit all around her.

As though she is the monster and hers is the cave.

The glinting, the glare of their lenses shatters in through her visor, all the brighter, all the worse for that. Her eyes are wet behind the metal and her vision swims with blue-green and orange-brown splotches. She's struggling to see.

Yet again, she will have to take off her helmet.

Though her hoody still covers her ears, the laughter seems somehow louder. The boy stands proud at the front of the pack, pointing at her with the index finger of one hand and with his phone too big and too flat in the other.

The rest ape his behaviour.

It takes her back to the playground.

The chanting.

The name.

She hates them.

She doesn't want to save them.

She shouldn't have come.

She should have taken her father's final advice.

No chance for that now, though.

Within the laughing faces, there's one that she knows. Again to the playground, hands pulling her hair. Hands that she recognises, bigger and older, wrapped round a phone, recording forever this dreg of a quest. This poor lonely knight errant with no sword and no helmet and no coat of arms, and her mystery utterly, totally stripped.

She turns away from him, from all of them.
Feels the shutter clicks clatter her armour like spears.

She starts to run, to sprint, panting over and over: I'm a knight, I'm a knight – but all the metal and foil of her shakes as she does so, and no longer keeps the same rhythm.

After she's gone, the pigeons return.

10

Nobody, thought Donna Crick-Oakley, had ever had such a shitty time of it while dressed up in armour.

She hadn't stopped running until she got back to her tower block. Not even when she reached the crossing.

Once she got into the lift, once the doors had closed, grindingly as ever, she found herself alone, properly this time, and buckled into a crouch, gasping for breath. She could taste bile or acid like bad orange juice in her throat. She had a stitch in her side, and she was burningly aware that she needed to weep. Wanted to disappear beyond camouflage into these mirrored steel walls.

She tried to hold off until she got home but, one floor before the top, her tear ducts gave way.

She sprinted across the landing, ignoring the stitch, but then it took her nearly a minute to open the door. She was sobbing so hard she kept dropping the keys.

The two baking trays and the pizza tray sat scrap-heaped on the worktop.

The helmet, such as it was, lay upturned on the floor.

She'd peeled off most of the duct tape, but remnants of the dark, gummy adhesive were still there, like a stain. It would come off with washing, Donna hoped, but perhaps not first time. Would probably hang around the way that grease did when she'd cooked potato smiles or breadcrumbed chicken pieces. It was a failure that she could be tasting for days.

11

Donna Crick-Oakley went through phases with her drinking.

When she'd been seventeen and freshly moved out from her mother's house, she had fallen in with a crowd who met at least twice a week in the park beside the church: they downed cheap vodka and alcopops and cans of cider that, even then, had tasted far too sickly sweet.

When some of them left for University, and the rest had simply decided that it was better to spend more money and go out to clubs as soon as they were able, Donna had slacked off on the booze and gone back to her books. The few nights that she had gone out, she'd usually met some guy or another. Sometimes they'd been guys that her friends had been wanting.

When they no longer invited her – except for the occasional group invite online – she took to buying a couple of bottles of wine a month, sometimes three. Sometimes four.

Maybe two nights a week, she would pour herself a few small glasses while she read, and snack on spiced cheese and olives that she'd picked up from the supermarket.

This had increased during the four-month period she was seeing Kirk. Probably, she'd started thinking after he left her, because being around him so often made her value her alone time all the more. And also because he enjoyed neither wine nor olives, and would only touch cheese when it was on a pizza, or a sub.

Earlier, once the sobbing subsided, she'd pulled the stopper out of this week's bottle, intending, mostly, just to finish it off.

She was halfway through the next one now, and already eyeing the one after that.

She sat squashed down into the beanbag, which she kept in her lounge area in lieu of an armchair, and looked lazily out through the balcony window.

Her glass was out of reach, on the shelf where she'd left it as she searched for a book, so she just swigged the wine straight from the bottle.

The book was half-beneath the beanbag, the reading abandoned after only a handful of pages.

She'd thought that maybe she could hide there, in the yellowed dunes of those pages, in the labyrinth-wall angles of their letters and words. But it turned out that she couldn't.

Not really.

Not today.

Standing, which was made harder not only by the quicksand-sagging of the beanbag but by the tiredness in her muscles from running and the wooziness that set in with the wine, she made her way over to the small desk that she kept to the right of the window. She leaned on it, palms flat, and drew the ugly, fire-retardant curtains closed.

She dropped into the old pneumatic chair.

The gas had long since left the mechanism, and so she dropped low.

She was only just above eye-level with her laptop now. It was as silver as her knightly armour had been, and she flipped open the lid to take her mind off of that.

It was dark like that shop, like that cave, for a moment.

The computer sputtered and whirred into life. The wallpaper was a picture of the kind of castle that slightly mad Bavarians used to build. It took four minutes for all of the icons to load up on top of it, and by that time she'd forgotten why she even turned it on.

Regardless, it hadn't helped. She was still thinking of armour. Thinking now of a coat of arms also.

Thinking how that castle would be part of it, probably. And possibly a wine bottle, or maybe more classically a big bunch of grapes.

And books, obviously. There always had to be books.

The browser opened at her homepage, her online bookstore *du jour*. Always.

She had a quick glance at the latest suggestions, the latest ideas the algorithm tried to plant in her head, but she didn't think that she'd buy anything, even when this tipsy. This fuzzy. This pished.

It wasn't so much that she was trying to cut down – if need be, she could always squeeze another bookcase in the kitchen, next to the fridge, and maybe one by the door – but rather that she wasn't sure about all these new writers that they were trying to promote, and she already had all the books – sometimes several editions – by most of the authors she truly admired.

Instead of risking something that might not be any good, or not quite good enough, she had decided now to hunt down more of the books that had inspired her favourite authors, though in many cases these weren't so easy to come by.

Time, almost inevitably, had winnowed their numbers.

That was why she relied more on second-hand shops: they sometimes got lucky.

And second-hand books, there was more experience in them, more history, that was another thing: there was more faith. More loyalty, as there was in an old dog. If it had been read and re-read and re-read until tattered, then it was more likely to be worth her reading as well.

41

Some of the new covers *were* eye-catching, though...

Clicking off, avoiding temptation, she moved onto her social network page.

She didn't visit it often, and when she did, it seemed as though there was always someone else she'd used to hang around with who'd got pregnant, or given birth, or got married, or taken a holiday somewhere with impossibly blue skies and improbably white sands; the pictures of which they'd nonetheless felt the need to apply a filter to, in order that they emerged even more blue and white still.

She never Liked them, those pictures.

She had seen better, she told herself.

She tried not to admit that they made her think of her dad.

She kept scrolling down.

Down.

Down.

Beyond all of that. Beyond cat videos and clickbait controversial opinion pieces about house prices, and immigration, and which cosmetics were reputed to be killing you slowly this week, or which superfood would keep you slim and trim and virtually immortal. Beyond all these signs of a life she didn't much want to lead.

And that's where she saw it.

Another photograph. This time of herself. Looking doe-eyed and startled, scared and ashamed. Helmet hanging impotently in her left hand. Right hand reaching upwards, too slowly, in a last vain effort to cover her face.

At least no filter was needed: with the sun on the foil, it was shiny enough.

Donna noticed the name of the person who'd uploaded it.

She hadn't read that name for so long, she'd all but forgotten she was friends with him on here. He obviously hadn't got pregnant or married or swanned off abroad. She probably hadn't thought of him since she'd accepted his Friend request, a couple of years back.

Until she'd spotted his face in the crowd this morning.

He'd been a peripheral figure in the group she'd gone drinking with in the park. That was how she'd first come back into contact with him. Though, in truth, they'd barely exchanged more than a few words a night.

Before that, though – long before that – they had been in primary school together.

Working through her memory now, she thought it quite likely that he'd been her first crush.

Looking at his profile picture, she wondered what she could have seen in him, all those ages ago.

After all, he was the one who'd come up with the nickname that followed her, on and off, from the last two years of primary school and all throughout secondary: Donna Creosote.

Because, as a nine year-old, she hadn't known what creosote was, she hadn't understood what he found so funny. When she'd asked her dad about it, and he'd told her it was used to paint fences, she'd understood even less.

None of the other kids had known what it was either, but that hadn't stopped them from laughing and chanting it whenever she walked by. On top of the chants and the jokes about her hair being ginger.

She found out later that Sammy himself only knew what it meant because his own dad was a landscape gardener.

Which, she found out later still, was code for him being an outdoorsy odd-job man.

She moved from his profile picture back to the image of her, defenceless in her armour. Despite the heavy coat of booze she'd replaced it with, Donna Creosote felt her face flush red and her eyes begin to sting.

She opened the 'Send Message' tab.

Bastard, she typed.

Dizzy, and with a rising sickness circling her tummy, she slumped on the edge of her bed. She'd taken her top off, but not her work trousers, and was too unsteady to risk heading over to the wardrobe for a clean pair of pyjamas.

Too unsteady to bend down and take off her socks.

She could see two chandeliers swinging above her, and the marble seemed slanted and slippy and cold.

12

The pages of the book were damp and warping. The sticky tape was coming away from the spine.

Donna hadn't put it back behind the curtain yesterday, and didn't notice that she'd left it out on the cistern until after she'd showered.

Sitting on the toilet, she wiped the cover with her towel, but doing so only seemed to spread the condensation, not remove it. She gave up, and riffled the pages: they sprayed droplets like a dog coming out of the rain.

She turned away. Tracking the motion so closely was making her queasy.

Without looking, there was a sound like rustling leaves.

She picked a page at random and smoothed it with a prune-skinned palm. Traced back and forth along the lines with fluctuating focus; squinting at the longer words, the several-syllable constructions.

There were two words, however, that came through quite clearly.

Tower

and

Princess.

They locked her eyes firm and stopped the world spinning.

It could be, she reflected, somewhat fuzzily, that she'd gone about her questing plans the day before in entirely the wrong way. It was quite possible, all things considered, that she simply wasn't built to be a knight.

Not because she didn't have a penis, or broad shoulders, or hair on her chest and spots on her back.

But because her brain seemed to glow whenever a princess was mentioned, even more so than it did when she read about knights.

They were almost sacred, to Donna. They weren't so much anachronistic as they were timeless, transcendent. They didn't need to belong, because they were above everyone anyway. They weren't burdened by doubts about their place in the world, didn't always have to gallivant about the countryside, waving their lances, desperate to prove it.

If she could be one of them, she thought, then her own worries would fade.

If.

Whenever she watched Disney films, though, it wasn't just the design of the heroic male characters that irked her, but that of the heroines as well. They were all nicely-drawn, and styled to appeal to children and vaguely-pervy blokes alike. But there was one abiding flaw, to Donna's mind, in each of them.

Not a one of them looked anything like her.

Her naked self in the mirror.
Not the fairest of them all.
Still a sheen of shower-water on her skin.
Ginger hair not yet blow-dried.
Legs not shaved for a fortnight.

Pubis a tangle of bright burnt sienna.

Those stretchmarks above her sharp-edged hips.

Despite the shower, a small tuft of t-shirt lint holding out in her navel.

Breasts not more than a handful. Despite the nakedness, nipples not cold, not hard, not perky. The room, with a bookcase blocking the window, was too close to sauna-hot for that.

Or perhaps the near-fever was another after-effect of the wine.

Her lips still had some redness on them, regardless of how much she'd scrubbed with a flannel, and then with her toothbrush, after she'd done scraping purple from her tongue and her teeth.

She closed her eyes.

Her brain bobbed and whorled in the pickle-jar murk.

She tried to swim alongside it, ride the current, take hold of it like a mermaid or a life-ring and float. Tried to grasp an image of herself in a tiara, in a shimmering satin ball gown, with matching gloves pulled halfway up along her freshly graceful arms. Her hair precisely curled and ornamental in its elegance. Her feet – no longer too big – slipped into dainty, cut-glass slippers with high heels that didn't hurt and that she could dance in, for a change. If anyone should ask.

And beneath that regal glitz, a body beautiful.

Beneath that gown, a pair of knickers that didn't have a picture on the front.

She chose the Pocahontas ones today.

47

She pulled on odd socks: one green with shocking pink diamonds, the other red with yellow smiley faces. Her mother had bought her both pairs last Christmas, ignoring the fact that she'd asked for a book.

She pulled the faded jeggings up along her stubbled calves, her stubbled thighs.

She pulled the blue-and-white-striped boob-tube down over her head, hoiked it into place above her navel – from which the lint had now been plucked – and below the collarbone she didn't care for, and which showed too clearly both her thinness and the propensity for accidents that had plagued her in her youth.

Sometimes, I swear you do this just to get attention.
So her ever-attentive father had said.

Donna stared with scarcely-hidden disappointment at the image in the mirror.

Thought of the money her father had left her.

Decided that, yes, she could definitely still afford to go shopping for clothes.

13

The kitchen-cum-lounge looked like a siege engine had hit it.

Still feeling shell-shocked herself, she narrowly avoided standing on the de-handled pan, but the cheese-grater on the front took a sizeable bite from the dry skin of her heel and made her jump to the table, where she banged her hip on a chair.

The oven trays seemed to tilt at her, mocking her, threatening to fall off the worktop and clatter and crash.

On the front of the fridge were some magnetic letters, a few of them rearranged into *buy sum more vvine!*

She moved to scramble them hurriedly, taking pains as she did so to avoid the empties by the bin.

As though they were peasants. Or lepers.

Or just suspicious old hags.

Pausing once again beside the table, aiming to regain her balance, she surveyed the remainder of the damage with a defeated general's eye: she saw the flattened beanbag, and another bottle beside it; the book underneath it, and the empty glass that occupied that book's place upon the shelf.

And the laptop. Lid open. Screen Whitby-Jet-dark.

Had she really been on it?

The word *Bastard* seemed to buzz on repeat at her fingertips. Beneath the nails that could probably do with being cut. With having those calcium-lack speckles glossed over, obscured.

Still unsteady from the booze, she poured herself a glass of water. Lukewarm and unfiltered, direct from the tap.
In
three
gulps
it was finished, and she was off across the flat.

As she waited for the computer to start up, for the icons to load, Donna thought about the castle in the middle of the screen. About the fantasy and patience it must have taken to construct a thing like that.
About the talent of the architect.
About the fervour of the builders.
About the majesty – the only word, really – of the views that might be seen from any given window. About how she'd never been inside the place to know those views for sure.
How she didn't even know if the entrance hall *was* marble.
How she wasn't even certain that she wanted it to be.

Those thoughts evaporated, however, once the whirring quieted down, and she could get back on her browser and check exactly what she'd done.

The echoes in her fingertips hadn't been lying.

But that wasn't the only thing she could see.

She noticed also – couldn't fail to – that the bastard had sent a message back.

Dear donna

i'm sorry for the picture and for tagging you in it.
I have untagged it now and taken it down and its
deleted from my phone as well... I didn't know it
was you when i was laughing. And I wasn't really
laughing at you really...I thought it looked kind of
weird and cool. The helmet was good, was brillan
tand when you took it off I took a picture because
I was surprised because I hadn't seen you in ages,,
and i think now i've seen you I miss you. you can
probably tell that I'm drunk I know but I honestly
am sorry and i miss you and the others as well...
do you see then much? I wasn't with anyone when
I Was in town....I didnt know anyone else who was
laughing. I don't ha\ve the picture anymore but i
guess that I took it because I never expected anyone
to do anything likc thata round here...I thought
it was only Americans who did superhero cosplay
stuff. Were you a robot... i'm sorry im drunk.

I'm sorry.

From

Sammy Pankhurst

Donna remembered that she had written him a letter once.
In primary school.
It had been three lines long.
She had ended it with *lots of love.*

He had taken great pleasure in reciting its contents to the
class, and any other kids who'd gathered round, in the cold of
the playground at break-time.

Had taken even more in wrapping up that reading with an ad-libbed *Creosote*.

Do you want to meet for coffee later? she replied.

She waited.

She'd be heading into town anyway, to buy herself a ball gown, and taking a break for coffee after all that hassle might be just what she needed.

Also, despite what he'd said about her armour, she felt that she should probably explain herself a little better. So as he didn't think her too weird. Or too lonely. Or too mad.

And what he'd said about the people from the old days, she understood the way he wondered how and where they were. She'd never really liked them much – or him, when she encountered him again, all those years after primary school and her first fairy-story broken heart – but she missed them all, and him, regardless. Sometimes.

Heedless of the lessons of the past, she longed for that past to return.

...boats against the current... wasn't that how it went?
A fairy tale, Donna thought, just with billboards and jazz.
A sad one.

On one of her shelves, perhaps in the bathroom.

Sammy replied: *ok... when's good for you?*

It was just after 11.

How about 2:30?

Ok... where?

The café at the far end of the Kingsgate.

ok... .see you there!!

As the machine began to power down, the icons left the background clear for just a moment.

Then it all went blue.

Then it all went black.

14

The lift stopped on the tenth floor. The doors opened, grindingly as ever, and there in the space between them stood a woman with a pram.

The same woman as yesterday, albeit dressed slightly differently.

Which, Donna supposed, she might be thinking as well.

Although, if the woman did recall her face, if not her jeggings and her boob-tube, and the loose purple cardigan she'd pulled on to keep her arms warm, then there was nothing in her expression or demeanour to show it.

The baby seemed to remember, though.
It started to cry.

The woman didn't spend the journey groundwards staring at Donna, not this time around.

But neither did she make any move to quiet her child, or to comfort it. The dummy had fallen out of its mouth and now rested on its chest, but the baby had been strapped in so tightly that its tiny fingers couldn't reach to put it back.

Nobody in the tower block besides that woman and her child had ever, for all Donna knew, properly seen her, at least not up close, whether dressed like this, or in knight's armour, or not. She thought about that, as the woman headed once more in the opposite direction.

She had made no effort to fit in, but neither had any of her neighbours gone out of their way to invite her to the house parties they frequently held. Despite the fact that she wasn't asked to them, she always knew when they were happening. She stood out on her balcony some nights and looked down at other balconies on the row across from hers, watching the washing lines and the plant pots and the birdshit-spattered plastic chairs, and the people sitting on them, smoking, drinking, laughing, and she heard their music turned up loud.

Whether she knew the songs that played or not, whether she liked the songs that played or not, she found she couldn't help but start to dance. She would dance by swaying her hips as she held onto the balcony rail. White-knuckled. She would let go of the rail sometimes and let her hips sway wilder, and, as she did so, she'd hope that no-one from the party looked up and saw.

Socially speaking, it probably wasn't the best way for a person to live.

But perhaps for a princess.

At the traffic lights, she once again followed the green angel's advice.

There were no car horns today.

If there had been, she would have thought of them as trumpets, heralding her approach.

Or tried to.

No pigeons fled at the sight of her, when she reached the other side.

If they had, she would have thought of them as doves, released into the sky to mark her coming coronation.

Or tried to.

55

In that empty window, however, she seemed anonymous, like the proverbial pauper before trading places. Or like a sacrifice left by the townspeople to placate whatever monster dwelt inside. Selected for her purity, no doubt, and her impeccable virtue.

If only.

Although the woman from her tower block hadn't appeared to recognise her, Donna was worried that the rest of those townspeople might. That they would laugh again to see her like this, as if defeated, disgraced.

As though they were the same crowd every day, and they occupied the same positions. On permanent lookout for wankers to mock.

Yet she walked all along New Street without being accosted, nobody grabbing her arm to say *Hey, didn't you...?* or *Where's your lance gone?*

No-one even looked twice.

She pulled her cardigan tighter about her, embracing it like a kind of invisibility cloak.

This was good, she supposed.

Better than she could have hoped for.

To have been let off so lightly.

Although she was a little put out that there wasn't even a flicker of yesterday's fire. Some trace of the embers, of charcoal, a remembrance daubed on the pavement. *Donna woz ere.* That might have been nice. After all, to judge by what Sammy said, it wasn't every day that someone walked through Huddersfield in full-on knightly armour.

Still, at least this way there was less chance of her being hassled in shops.

In the first of the shops, she couldn't find anything she wanted. That is, she found several things she fancied trying on, but none that were tied into her quest for a gown. If it hadn't been quarter-past one already, she might have considered it. As it was, there was no time to waste.

In the next shop she checked, the story was the same. No decent prom dresses or ball gowns, despite or perhaps due to it being the season, so she didn't hang around to browse their other wares.

The shop after that was a charity one, devoted to helping the needy in Africa, and while Donna didn't really expect to find anything much in the way of regal attire, she stepped inside anyway and homed in on the books.

The bulk of them today were either thrillers, which she didn't really read, or cheap romance novels, which usually contained a different kind of fantasy to that which she preferred. No battered spines or sticky-tape stood out to her today, much less roused her pity.

Besides, there was no time to waste.

It was twenty-five to two now, and she had no idea how that had happened.

With her mother it would have been different. Donna didn't trust her mother's fashion sense as far as she could throw it, but found she was missing her input, her ideas, her efficiency, all the same. Her presence, even. Which was especially surprising.

Though whether good or bad surprising wasn't clear yet.

In the next place, the big multi-floor mega-chain at the far end of town, she could have filled several bags easily, just with everyday things. But the queues were too long. If she wasn't careful, she could end up stuck in there for hours: the worst kind of labyrinth, the kind where you could see the way out but couldn't reach it.

She didn't like queueing, particularly not on her own. To cope with the boredom, she always ended up getting things she didn't really need; falling hook, line and sinker for their impulse-buy bait. If it wasn't fluffy slipper-socks, it was tiny teddy bear keychains, or glittery scrunchies, or multipacks of underwear adorned with cuddly cartoon animals rather than mass-market fairy-tale faces. Which turned out to be children's sizes and which, having tried a pair on, she'd had no choice but to discard.

None of which, she feared, would be a good enough reason to stand someone up.

She hadn't wanted to look for owt in Kingsgate, because she hadn't wanted to run the risk of Sammy spotting her, seeing what she was buying and thinking her even weirder still. And now the quickest way down there would take her back through that square, like revisiting the site of a battle she'd lost. But it didn't really seem as if there was anything else for it.

The closer she got, the more she wished she had bought something, anything, from that last shop, so she'd have one of their trademark brown paper bags now to hide herself, her burning face, as she passed. She couldn't really remember the last time that she'd felt so embarrassed in public.

Walking past the Library, it seemed as though the statues that framed the steps were embarrassed by her too. Mortally ashamed, distancing themselves after her failed fantasy coup. One of them even had his eyes rolled back in his head.

She hurried onwards, keeping her own to the ground.

It was only when she arrived at the shopping centre that she stopped again to look up. The unseasonable sun streamed in through the skylights, bounced off the pale flooring and made the place glow.

For a moment, it lit up a shop window ahead as though gracing stained glass, conjuring angels and the ghost of the Grail.

Her breath caught at the thought of the ultimate quest.

Then an old woman clipped Donna's left heel with a shopping trolley, and a young boy banged into her right knee and wheeled away crying, prompting his father to spin round and give her the muckiest look.

I'm sor–

But they were already gone.
Lost in the rush.

Donna blinked and saw haloes.

She followed them forwards, found her way to the shop.

There were three silver mannequins, decked out in long dresses. These were satin and boldly coloured and reached nearly to the floor, as Donna felt the dress of any proper princess should. Not entirely to the floor was best, as it left ample space for showing off one's tastefully bejewelled shoes.

Inside, she could only find two of the showcased dresses in her size, but this hardly lessened her excitement. Ignoring the disparaging glances of the girl behind the till, she escorted both into the changing room and took her own sweet time to try them on.

The first was light blue and she adored the way it hung almost curvaceous on her hips. But the colour blended, oddly, too closely to her skin and made it appear even more pasty than usual, and so, after *umming* and *ahhing*, she had to discard it.

The second was a deeper, darker tone: a bold, almost racing green. While it too made her skin look pale, it was the milky-smooth pallor that Donna associated with princess-style pampering, with being waited on hand and foot by a dutiful network of nurses and maids.

It didn't relieve the sharpness of her hips the way the blue one had, unfortunately, but it would still make a great start to her royal collection.

Wearing it had made her feel better already.

Just the closeness to its fabric, draped tenderly across her forearm, seemed to lend her a confidence she usually lacked. As she approached the till – at which, mercifully, there wasn't a queue – she met the assistant's piggy-eyed gaze without blinking.

The assistant accepted the dress with a sneer – barely concealed, though she seemed caked in concealer – and inspected the price tag as though the transaction was all an elaborate scam, and she was in no way about to be caught.

When Donna paid, calmly, with her debit card, the assistant's face fell.

She handed the bag over.

I'll put the receipt in here, she said, recovering slightly. *In case you have to return it.*

Donna simply smiled. The envy of commoners never ceased to amaze her.

Walking out of the shop, she could feel her blood rushing – her first princess gown since the pink and gold one she'd worn to bits as a kid – and she really quite wanted to go find some shoes.

But it was twenty-past two, and there was no time to waste.

15

Romance, to nine-year-old Donna Crick-Oakley, had meant being sent to bed early, whenever her parents had wanted a night to themselves. It had meant hearing the music, the soppy old ballads, coming up through the floor like hot air, like helium. It had meant listening to a book on tape, or reading aloud to herself to cover the noise.

It had meant being left out.

It had meant never really knowing what was going on downstairs.

Nobody told her, and she wasn't sure how to ask.

Some of the stories she read or listened to on such nights were about true love, of course. But she understood the bond between lovers only as that between the seeker and the sought, the hunter and the hunted. It was a question of purpose. A matter of want.

We just want some peace and quiet tonight, for a change, her parents would say.

Although she was never quite convinced that this met the requirements.

True love, to nine-year-old Donna, had seemed something grander, much more ambitious: the finding of treasure, reaching the goal at the end of a quest.

Prince Charming, for example, only found his true love when he found the foot that fitted the glass slipper.

Beauty found her true love when she found a way to turn the Beast back into a man.

When Donna first began to take notice of Sammy Pankhurst, however, she did not think he was a treasure.

As a nine-year-old himself, only two months older than she was, he had been a shambles of curly dark hair and red cheeks and white, crooked teeth. He looked nothing like the characters in Disney films, not even the baddies. He looked nothing like she pictured any of the characters in her books.

Except sometimes, she thought, like Pinocchio, when he'd been turned into a donkey.

She thought that when he picked on her. Which he seemed to do whenever he was able, especially after he coined the nickname that amused him so much.

It wasn't just chanting, though, like the rest of her class. He had pushed her into walls as well, and, when she dobbed him in to the teachers, he'd blamed it on other boys and got away without punishment. He had frequently sent her notes in class informing her that she smelled, and timed their being passed to her so expertly that she got the blame for them, rather than him.

Though she had not been familiar with the word at the time, she'd thought young Sammy Pankhurst was a right little bastard.

And yet.

And yet.

She had wanted to be near him.

Grown-up Sammy Pankhurst did not look the same as he had then. He didn't even look much like his profile picture, cropped out from a group shot of them all in the park. Gone were the dark curls and the red cheeks, replaced by a short, unshowy quiff and a neat layer of stubble, which suited him unexpectedly well.

As he approached her table now, she thought there was even a kind of swagger about him. A strut. An easiness. A physical confidence that he hadn't exactly exuded on those cold nights in the park, and perhaps not back in the playground either, popular though he'd been.

Some kids had played tag in that playground, and some had played house. Some kids just ran around with their Action Men or their My Little Ponies; others hopped around making horsey noises, or rolled about miming machine guns, plosive, explosive, tongues against teeth.

She had wanted Sammy to help her play Little Red Riding Hood – he could be the wolf or the woodcutter, whichever he chose – but the one time she managed to ask him, he just pushed her and called her the name and ran off.

She wasn't sure, as she watched him, what she wanted right now.

16

H ello.

Hey, Donna.

So, how are you?

I'm good. Thanks. Yourself?

Good, thanks.

Ok.

Ok. Ok.

What would you like to drink? Would you like a drink?

What?

A drink. Would you like one?

Cappuccino, please. Medium.

Ok.

    Donna watched him queuing.
    He was behind four other people.

He seemed to have more patience with it than she would have had.

Thank you. What did you go for?

A latté.

Ok. You say it *lah-tay?*

Yeah.

That's always sounded kinda posh to me. Have you been living down south, or–

No. That's just how I say it. I thought that was how people said it.

I guess it's sort of like scone and scon.

When people ahead of me in line order lattés, they always say it like that.

Do you say it like, you know, bone, or do you say it like scon? I've always said scon, because me and my grandma, my dad's mum, we always had this joke when I was younger about how, when I'd eaten mine really quickly – because she always had at least one waiting for us whenever we'd visit, you know – I'd say, 'Look, s'gone!', and I liked the way she laughed at that. She couldn't eat hers quickly, though, because she said it gave her heartburn, and it played heck with her dentures.

I think that's just the right way to say it.

What is? Scon?

No, I was talking about lattés.

Oh.

I say scon too, though.

Ok.

How have you been, anyway? What have you been up to? Do you still–

Just hold up there. That's a lot of questions all at once.

Sorry. It's just been a while.

S'ok.

Ok.

I'm alright, though. I've been alright. I've been... I've not been doing too much, I don't suppose. Bits and pieces. I had a kind of data entry job thing, but it didn't last. It was only temp work, you know.

Yeah.

But I don't really need the money at the minute. You know, after my dad left and everything.

Oh, right. I thought I remembered something about that, but wasn't sure. It's been – how long has it been?

Four, four-and-a-half years.

Feels like longer.

Yeah, sometimes.

Do you ever hear from your Dad, by the way?

Let's not talk about that, please.

Ok. Ok, sorry.

It's ok. How are you, anyway? What have you been up to? I feel a bit rude not asking –

It's ok. I'm working at the market on weekends now. You know I used to work on Wednesdays? Do you remember the stall I used to work in?

Vaguely, I think.

Well, it's not that one that I work at anymore, but it's similar. Because you know how I used to be a butcher, well, I didn't used to be a butcher, but I worked at the butcher's stall.

Yeah.

Well, I work at the fishmonger's now. And I'm getting proper training so as I can prepare all the fish, like, every species – is 'species' the right word to use for fish? – every type of fish, anyway, that we sell. So, I'll be able to prepare it, is the idea, as well as just selling it.

That's good, then. That's – cool.

Yeah. Do you eat much fish?

Not too much. But sometimes I like to cook with it. And salmon, like smoked salmon, that's really good with cream cheese.

Well, we sell salmon, smoked and unsmoked. Fillets and things. And, like, everything else you could want, really, I guess, so come down to our stall if you want any. The next time you want any, just come down at a weekend and ask for me and I'll get you what you want.

Promises, promises.

Thanks. Thank you, that's very nice of you, Sam.

Sammy.

Sammy. Sorry.

No worries. Also, one of the things we notice, me and Jim, the guy who owns the stall, one of the things we notice is that a lot of people seem to buy fish mainly to put in pies.

Oh?

Yeah. But they always, when they buy the fish, they always ask us what's the best way to cook it in a pie. What the best ingredients are, you know, what the best herbs are, what the best kind of sauce to use with it is, whether or not it should have this kind or that kind of potato in, you know – and the thing is, so many people ask us that, me and Jim, that we had this idea. Sometimes it's even people who've asked us before who'll ask us about it – they'll ask us, 'We made a pie like you said last time, and it was really tasty, but we can't remember what you told us to put in it, you know, and we fancy another.' – and so many people ask us for our suggestions that we've decided we're just going to start selling our own.

Your own pies? That, yeah, that sounds like a good idea.

Yeah. Yeah, it's a really good idea, because, like I say, people keep asking about our recipe, so we've decided to just give them our recipe direct. You know, as a pie, like. Because that's what our customers want, Jim says. Convenience.

Yeah.

Convenience and quality, that's what Jim says. And our pies'll be quality, and it'll be convenient because people won't have to cook their own from scratch, and they won't have to ask us for the recipe every time. So it's a win-win, you know? We haven't decided yet whether we're going to pre-prepare some every weekend, like you see in supermarkets, or if we're going to offer like a pie-on-demand service — that's what Jim's thinking of calling it, 'Pie-on-Demand' — where people would be able to order a pie in mid-week, say, and then pick it up on Saturday, ready for eating that night, like after the match or something.

Oh.

Yeah, it's a really good idea. I think we'll go with 'Pie-on-Demand', because it's what people want, really. Sets us apart from the supermarkets, makes it feel like they're getting value for money, you know. And gives them control, kind of thing. The personal touch, Jim calls it.

Yeah, I can see why that would appeal.

Yeah.

Yeah. It's a good idea.

He smiled at that, and she noticed that his teeth were still pretty white and not all that crooked.

Do you like pies? Fish pies, I mean? Because we're doing a test-run of Pie-on-Demand this next weekend, I think, but we haven't announced it on the stall yet, so if you get your order in now, we can get you fixed up before anyone else. I can try to get you a discount too, if you'd like?

Erm, I don't really like pies, no. I'm sorry. I don't like the pastry. When it's hard, it's all flaky and gets stuck to the roof of my mouth, and when it gets soggy it just tastes – it just doesn't taste very nice to me.

Do you not even like admiral's pies?

No, I'm sorry.

Do you know which ones they are? They really don't have pastry. There's sometimes a bit, round the sides, but the top part's all potato. Mashed potato, sometimes with cheese. You said you liked cheese, right?

Yeah, I like cheese, but I'm not really too keen on the mash, either. Sorry.

Oh, right.

I'm sorry. I'm sure they are really good, if you like that kind of thing.

They are. It's ok.

Thanks for the coffee, though.

It's ok, no worries.

Ok.

Anyway –

The smile was gone now. The cheeks were a little red again.

Yeah?

Do you ever see any of the others? Do you go out with them or anything?

I did, for a while, but haven't seen any of them for over a year or so now, I don't think.

Oh. That's a shame. That's not good.

Well, it is how it is. How about you? Do you ever see them?

No. Not really, no.

Ah.

It was hard to keep in touch, when they went off to uni and things, you know?

Yeah.

I'll message them from time to time, and ask how they are, but I don't get many replies.

Yeah.

I wanted to try and arrange a meet-up over Christmas. It didn't come off, though. I sent a message round to everybody – didn't you get it?

No, I don't think I did.

Oh, maybe I didn't send it to you, then. If that's the case, sorry. I must just have forgot, I didn't mean it as if I didn't want you to come or anything.

It's ok. You don't have to say sorry all the time.

Ok. I'm thinking of trying to arrange another meet-up for the summer, so I'll invite you to that, definitely. I figure that, because it isn't Christmas, people shouldn't have so much family stuff to do, family parties and things, so it should be easier to find a time that everyone can make, you know?

Hopefully.

She sipped at her cappuccino, but it was just the foam on the bottom that was left. His latté was nearly gone, too, though she couldn't think when he'd had time to drink it. She licked the foam off her lip.

He watched her.

I'm sorry about yesterday, by the way.

It's ok, it was a misunderstanding. Don't worry about it.

Ok, but I am sorry. I didn't know it would hurt you so much to put that picture up. And I didn't mean to laugh at you, really. I didn't know it was you. I was laughing with –

It's ok. Really.

Ok? Ok.

I think I'm going to go home now, though, because I've got a book club later, and I need to cook and eat beforehand and everything.

But this has been nice.

Thanks, it has. I'm glad you think so.

Ok.

And I was kind of thinking it would be good to do it again. You know, to keep in touch, to keep the spirit of the group together. Until we can all meet up in the summer, you know?

Ok.

Ok?

Ok. Well, I'd best be going. It was good to see you.

It was great to see you too. Hope you enjoy your book group.

Thanks. Enjoy your... good luck with your pies.

Thanks, Donna. See you soon.

Bye.

17

onna Crick-Oakley did not have a book group to go to.

What she did have was an odd feeling that she'd agreed to the possibility of seeing him again.

She quite wanted some wine, and to curl up in her dress.

18

Sitting on the edge of her bed, Donna studied her reflection. She stood and twirled, awkwardly, in the small space between.

How do I look? she asked the mirror.
Do I look like a princess?

It didn't reply.

She had showered for the second time that day. Beneath the waterfall, she'd shaved her legs. In the changing room, the dress had rubbed and caught against the stubble, but with her shins and knees and thighs all smooth it rested on those legs just fine.

No static.
No sparks.
Not even when spinning.

Though it remained uneasy on her hips, no matter how she tried to shape it with her hands. It fell into sharp and strange creases, as if those hips and the stretchmarks around them gave off a powerful magnetic field that couldn't be denied.

If only.

Still, she couldn't really complain at small niggles like that, not when it made such a difference to her complexion: it lent an almost airbrushed creaminess to her features and it made the green-brown colour pop more brightly from her eyes; it made her lips seem fuller, far more red. In throwing a little shadow on her cleavage, it made her breasts seem more than just a handful.

She cupped them, for a second.

She really did feel better in this dress. Sexier, even. Happier, too.

Was happiness equivalent to princess-hood?

How could she tell?

There were happy princesses in the books she'd read, of course, particularly in the ones that she'd read over and over. But there were miserable ones as well. Tragic cases. Damsels that remained very much in distress.

It was a long while, she realised, since she'd properly looked at a picture of a princess – the small plasticated prints of them on her knickers didn't count – and though she thought she'd had a pretty solid idea of them in her head, she found she was no longer quite certain how they should be.

Or whether a single dress, by itself, was a passable solution.

The silver, no-face mannequins that modelled them had hardly had a regal bearing. Hadn't sported any jewellery in particular, or worn those pointy hats that had at one time been the height of princess fashion.

Her first and only other princess dress had come with one of those – her mum made it from two empty tubes of kitchen roll, cut and artfully arranged together, with pink crepe paper draped around in place of silk.

Her mum made the rest of the dress as well. Stitched it together from bits of a blouse and an old satin dressing gown that was long past its best. Donna put it on sometimes, when they sent her upstairs. She had played out in the back garden with it, too, and been reprimanded for getting mud on the hem and a grass-stain down the side.

She had felt sometimes like an ugly sister, even though she was an only child.

The apparel doth oft proclaim the man, her dad used to say.

Bloody Shakespeare.

If she didn't fasten the top button on her school shirt in the morning and push her tie right up, her dad used to tell her off. Tell her that no daughter of his was going to leave the house dressed like a scruff.

If she had her shirt tucked out when he came to listen to her read, he'd ask, in deadly earnest, if she'd been like that all day.

It was possible that her own dress sense, her own habits, weren't quite up to scratch. That there might not be any way to fashion herself as a fairy tale princess without at least paying heed to the pictures she'd seen. Illustrations and photographs, Disney or not.

After all, that was the only way that her mother had been able to design the first one, wasn't it?

They had sometimes watched those films together, when her dad was out, at the football, or at an educational conference or a parents' evening, or a pub. Her mum had sometimes sung along, so loud that Donna couldn't hear the actors.

The house had been littered with picture books and, when Donna was four or five or six, with tracings of those pictures that she'd made herself. She would colour them in and then hold them up to a window, so that they shone like angels or martyrs or saints in stained glass.

Red and green. Other colours.

Some nights, her dad would come back late from work – another cause for argument – and arrive with a shopping bag holding even more books. After navigating the maelstrom of the kitchen, he would empty the contents carefully onto her bed like a pedlar displaying his wares, then shuffle them, and fan them out before her in his big, red-ink-stained hands.

Pick a card, any card...

One would always stick out more than the others, of course, and she gathered that this was the one he wanted to hear most himself. Sometimes she'd oblige; sometimes she wouldn't. It depended which future she thought looked the best.

Against the old adage, she judged by their covers.

At first, these gifts were chock-a-block with illustrations; then, as she grew, so these pictures diminished in quantity until there were only frontispieces, and then finally just the words.
Her intellectual evolution.
She went from holding up the pictures to show him, like her teacher did, displaying them like cavemen did with charcoal paintings, all the way to reading seriously, as if giving a speech in assembly, or delivering a eulogy in church, like her dad had given at her grandma's funeral.
In this latter phase, if she was reading a play, he'd often join in, insisting that they apportion the characters between them. He'd criticize her for not doing different voices, for the mispronunciation of certain words; he'd stop, at seemingly random intervals, to quiz her about the meaning of this or that archaic phrase.

Bloody Shakespeare.

It was about that time, she thought, that she must have taken more of a shine to maths. Enjoying the solitude of it, the pure mental engagement. The answers that were the same in any language, any age.

It was about then that she began to argue with her dad, telling him she'd much rather just read in her head.

Overhearing her mum: *She's a young woman now, Charles. She does need her privacy.*

She had been running away from those pictures for years because they denied her imaginative licence, because they never looked how she wanted them to. Which is, they never looked like her.

Now, she thought perhaps the problem might be on her side of the equation. That it was she who didn't look enough like them, because she'd never paid enough attention, because she'd turned her back on their example. Because – as both her parents would have said – she'd cut off her nose to spite her face.

She flopped back on her bed and rolled across it to the other side. Her eyes were closed as she did so, and her dress gave out a sound like the rustling of leaves, as if she was tumbling down a woodland knoll in autumn, gathering grass-stains.

Not that they'd show up much on this colour.

She kept her oldest books in the bookcase in the far corner of her room, well away from the door and the side of the bed where any male visitors would usually sleep. Forensically, archaeologically, she moved down through the strata, until she was crouched low enough to inspect the first shelf.

Her back resting against the bed, her gown bunched up above her knees so that she didn't catch or crease it on the lines between her bookish tiling, she stroked her fingertips across the lined-up spines like tracing cracks and whorls in bark. Her hands came back dusty, almost mossy, and she couldn't find anywhere to wipe it off. Her dress wouldn't do, and neither would the glossy covers underneath her. She reached behind her instead, rubbed it away on the not-quite-so-clean sheets.

Though she hadn't read any of these volumes in ages – probably hadn't even taken them out for a clean in eighteen months – Donna knew that they were the most obvious repositories for the images she wanted.

The ideas, as well.

The ideas for how she'd hold herself, alone and in potential company; for how she'd sit, and stand, and eat, in same. For how she'd be when she was merry, or uncertain, or afraid; for which shoes she'd wear, and what kind of jewellery might best accompany her dress; for what makeup, if any. The ideas for how she'd be and how she might best lean in to kiss, in proper princess style, the man who'd come to save her.

She blew and swept the dust from the tops and sides and lower edges of the books, each in turn, and flicked their pages open tenderly, as though they were as antiqued and battered as her poor second-hand strays, and hadn't in the first place been printed on thick, child-proof paper, strong almost as armour, with an equally tough outer shell.

She looked upon the pictures as though they'd been brought to her, been salvaged from an attic or a cellar or a vault someplace, a farmhouse, where they'd been given in lieu of payment for milk, or bacon maybe, in some more trusting long ago. As though they were oil paintings: old and cracked perhaps, but gorgeous in their mastery of form and neoclassical technique.

She wanted them to be that way, to mean that much.

She wanted to see them, without deception, how they'd appeared when she was reading with her father at her side.

In Cinderella's peasant garb, Donna discerned more than a little of her former self. In this particular version, the first five or six times that she appeared, Cinders wore a patched-up blue skirt that was fraying at the hem. Above, she wore a white blouse, with a hole at one elbow, and an apron, light caramel, like roughly tanned leather: closer to a blacksmith's outfit than to what Donna guessed would have been in vogue for servant girls back then.

In the glamorous confection she wore to the Prince's ball, however, Donna could see something of the self-image she longed for. This gown (shown across the next four pages) was pink, rather than the green that Donna was currently dressed in. But the style, minus the bustle at the back, was at least something similar, in that it stretched as closely to the ground as it could while still affording a little space for her glass slippers to show through and sparkle.

For all the cultural import of such footwear, Donna had yet to see any for sale on the High Street.

A slight wrinkle in her plans, perhaps, but not to worry.

The sequinned flats in her wardrobe would do for now.

Snow White's clothes were less openly suited to fancy party situations, but they represented, at least between the covers of this book, a more upmarket variation on older European daywear.

Possibly, Donna thought, in order to avoid embarrassment on a level with her knight errant escapade, she could adapt to something similar when she next went into town.

Beauty – that is, Belle – began this version of her tale dressed in much the same manner. But then just past the halfway point she moved into party-dress mode, being entertained as she was by the wild boar-like Beast. It was a multi-tiered red number, with white elbow-length gloves; a red ribbon in her hair, and a ruby rose pendant adorning her neck.

The dress was comparable to Donna's only in the depth and richness of its colour, but at least the necklace might have more present applications.

Rapunzel didn't really get to wear a ball gown.

Not in the children's book that Donna had.

But neither was she condemned to simply scabby peasant clothing. Rather, she wore what Donna could best equate to being the princessy equivalent of tracky bottoms and a hoody. A smart dress and sensible shoes, but without a bustle, or too much make-up, or a tiara. Which, while reflecting the fact that she was unaware of her lineage, remained the kind of thing that someone of such lineage might plausibly slob out in at the weekend, when taking a break from all other duties.

Only, Rapunzel had no other duties.

Her sole calling was to walk and sit and sleep within her small home at the top of a tower. Was to cradle her chin in her hands on the windowsill, while her long golden locks fluttered out in the breeze.

Waiting for a man to discover her, and to use those locks then as a ladder to climb.

In search of love.

True or not.

Waiting to pass, it could be said, from one form of captivity to the next.

Although, these stories seemed to say, was there much point in being a princess if you didn't wish to find a prince?

Indeed, at that book's closing, when she had done so, Rapunzel certainly looked happy.

And Donna felt, wanted to feel, that she could learn a lot from that picture about how a princess ought to smile.

There was still a slight hurdle, however, that stopped her believing she could ever quite be like them. Like Rapunzel and Cinders and Snow White and Belle. Those fantastical damsels.

It was a little thing, really, but it made a big difference.

Not one of those damsels had ginger hair.

19

I t was a good red.

Although, as she held it up to the light, it looked mainly dark inside the bottle, and the empty shoulders of the bottle glowed a sickly shade of green.

Champagne would have been more suitable, she guessed, but she didn't have any in, and besides, she didn't really like it. She just needed something, she felt, a bottle of something, to smash against the hull of this new part of her journey; to christen this dress, this new way of life.

Sitting there at the kitchen table, staring at the magnetic letters on the fridge, she became dimly aware that the landline was ringing.

She didn't go to answer it.

She knew who it was.

Her mother's voice sounded after the beep:

Hey love, it's only me, just seeing if you fancy going out for a carvery on Sunday? Or I could cook? It's been a while since I came round. Have you got rid of that beanbag yet? My place might be better. Bob's really looking forward to meeting you. And he's got a son about your age –

Donna didn't wait for the message to finish before walking over to the beanbag with her wine.

Her mother had only started seeing Bob about two months ago, after they crossed paths – so her mother had delighted in informing her – at a curry and karaoke night *down the local*. And Donna had no interest in either him or his progeny.

Her mother had been with several men over the past three years, but none had got as far as being invited to move in and so, given the rarity with which she visited anyway, Donna had managed to avoid running into them.

It wasn't that she didn't trust her mother's taste in men, she told herself.

Nor that she didn't want her mother to be happy.

And she'd given up, this far down the line, on having her father return. Either to the country, or to the North, or to her mother, or to her.

She just didn't want to be part of that happiness, or whatever it was that her mother kept finding.

Her mother didn't approve of the way Donna lived, the way she read so much, the way she cleaned or didn't clean. The way she kept bookcases in the bathroom. The way she had a beanbag instead of an armchair. The way she'd sold her TV. The way her flat was on the top floor, and the way she went out onto the balcony, which was totally unsafe. The way she dressed. The way she never even thought of doing something different with her hair, like dyeing it. The way she couldn't get, or didn't want, a steady job. The way she couldn't get a steady man, and kept on picking losers ('Bob's a winner, love. And so's his son.') The way she drank wine on her own –

She raised her glass again and sipped.

– The way she never went out and met new people.

And Donna, for her part, didn't approve of the way her mother lived, the way she didn't read, except for glossy, trashy magazines, and the way she cleaned so often that her house reeked not of lemons but of acrid *lemon fresh*. The way she only kept one thing beside the toilet, and the way that thing was *The Daily Star*. The way she'd kept an armchair that used to be Donna's gran's – *yes, Donna, s'gone* – and didn't sit in it but left it piled high and ragged instead with those shitty magazines. The way she stared at her TV screen so intently that anyone might think she'd had a sudden miraculous conversion and now saw the face of her lord and saviour in every soap and talent show. The way she'd traded in the family home, which Donna's father had been forced to leave her, for a bungalow two streets away and three doors down from a woman that she hated. The way she dressed. The way she was always doing something different with her hair, always picking out the latest style and colouring from fashion columns in the paper; her hair-dye history seemed, to Donna, like a rainbow re-envisioned by the criminally insane. The way she'd kept the same steady job for years, even though, or perhaps because, she harped on about it constantly. The way she'd found a string of men, but kept on dumping them, because, she said, she needed someone younger – a fate that Donna thought would befall Bob, too. And sooner rather than later.

The way she always went out and met new people, because the old ones didn't want to know.

Neither did Donna.

There was nothing even close to good enough for either of them around the other.

There hadn't been for quite some time.

20

Her sixth glass of wine sloshes round in her hand and her ball gown spills shimmering across the beanbag like oil.

Donna Creosote, however, doesn't watch the wine moving. Or the curtains shifting with the breeze between the balcony doors.

Her head lolls towards the nearest bookcase.

The titles on the spines there are beginning to dance, to tango in duplicate around their initial location. The leather of some of those bindings, the linen, the creases riven in the paperbacks seem almost like bark for a moment: oaky and thick, even dotted with lichen.

Fallen olives, from the jar that she's been snacking on, are littered between beanbag and shelving like acorns. Or breadcrumbs. At any rate, a path.

There are fresh shoots beside it. Saplings. The carpet all ruffled, like more earth being displaced.

She leans closer, squints, as if to follow where it leads.

A clearing in the archive, between boughs, where she'd removed a book earlier and not put it back. There's something inside it, but she's struggling to focus.

A gingerbread house?

A gathering of outlaws, all dressed in green?

No. It's a tree, the highest widest oldest tree in the forest, and carved on its trunk is a heart with an arrow shot through.

Her initials are there, maybe, on the top side of that arrow. But beneath it, who else's?

Not Bob's son's, that's for sure.

She doesn't want Bob's son, and she doesn't want Kirk, and she probably, definitely doesn't want Sammy. And she doesn't want any of the other boys she's had.

Because that's what they'd been, really: boys.

They'd seemed like adults, of course – like adults should be, as far as she knew. And all of them were older than her, which should have counted for something. But then they got childish again: they grew backwards as soon as she gave them attention.

When she hung out with men that she found herself attracted to, and they began to call her names, however jokingly, and tickle her, and began to be *boys*, when that happened Donna felt like she herself was nine or ten years-old again, and half-expected, whenever she walked past a wall with a *boy*friend, to be pushed into it.

Putting a hand out to steady herself – the graze on her palm.

They made her feel like a girl, and where did that leave them, then?

Just two kids in the forest, and that never ended well.

Innocents, lost.

Ever since her first time, ever since she'd discovered what it was all about, she had struggled to understand why people talked about sex as one of the things that made you grown up. It felt like the opposite: it was messy and smelly and loud and all the things you got told off for being when you were younger.

It was fun.

She liked it.

She couldn't help herself, sometimes.

But sometimes, it felt like she was a toy, a game, and they just wanted to play with her.

She'd known boys at school who'd do anything to play with their toys, of course. That wasn't necessarily bad. As she'd hungered for break-times, so had they, she'd seen it; they'd rushed to their bags in the cloakroom, desperate to get to their latest action figure, their latest car, running out to race them or fight them on the tarmac. They took the figures to the front gates, had them climb up the bars, in a bid to reach freedom.

One of them had cried all afternoon after dropping his favourite, a Batman, out through a gap, where it had fallen on the pavement and rolled into the road. He'd loved it that much.

And yet, there was a chance he'd only loved it because it was exactly how he'd wanted it to be. It had existed entirely in relation to him.

Even if that car hadn't come along, it would still have been abandoned eventually: put up in the attic, or given away as a hand-me-down for somebody else. If there was anyone else.

It would have stopped existing just as surely.

You couldn't rely upon that kind of love.

Leaving you stranded in the dark with the witch or the wolf.

Donna's done with all that. She wants to feel like a woman, full-grown, like she owns herself, like she has some kind of control over how things play out in her life.

That's all she's asking.

How that meshes with being sprawled out in a princessy dress upon a beanbag, drinking wine as though it's fizzy pop, she isn't quite sure.

She reaches out for one of those olives.

Belches.
Feels queasy.

Maybe, she thinks, she should get some fresh air.

21

The night sky over Huddersfield is like a ripening bruise. The sound of fighting sings loudly from one of the apartments below.

This isn't usually a worry that she has with her neighbours; she's seldom clued in on their problems and feuds.

But their shouts rise past her balcony tonight like fireworks. Leaving certain words behind them like different coloured sparks.

fucking
Blue.

idiot
Bronze.

I
White.

can't
Red.

Blue.

believe
Orange.

you
Yellow.

Blue.

snogged
Green.

him
Grey.

Like all the other firework displays she's seen, it quickly springs an ache in Donna's head.

She looks elsewhere, further out across town. Towards Castle Hill in one direction. Towards the football stadium in another. Sweeping white support bars above the blue roof like bones.

Her father had taken her to watch a match there once, when she was twelve. She remembered that he'd bought her a pie at half time and she hadn't liked it. It had been chicken and mushroom, and she didn't like mushrooms and she didn't like pastry. He hadn't asked her what she wanted before he went to buy it, but he should still have known because he was her dad.

Town had lost the match 3-2, to a late goal in injury time, and he didn't take her again.

After the final whistle had blown and they were walking out through the turnstiles into the car park, one of her father's friends – with whom he went, at that time, to every home game – had joked that she was bad luck.

She didn't much like football before that, which is why her father had waited until she was twelve. She hated it after.

She sways with her hands on the balcony rail, as she gazes back towards the town centre. Clubs are flaring up like bonfires, sending out smoke signals to call in the horny.

She should be there, she thinks.

She thinks that the bass they give off is like the heartbeat of some colossal creature in the distance. Or maybe two of them. Or maybe more. Ribcages the size of that which frames the football pitch. Cocks the size of Castle Hill.

This is how such mythical beasties are made.

This is how legends are brought into being.

But Donna doesn't go.

Instead, she keeps swaying.

She sways because she's drunk, and not because her neighbour's argument has a rhythm she can dance to.

She sways because she can't stand still.

It really is a long way down, she thinks.

A very long way indeed.

22

If I'm going to be a good princess, she thinks, then I should really grow my hair.

23

Since she was knee-high to a gnat, as her grandma used to say, Donna had been able to visualise settings extraordinarily well.

Reading through her first non-illustrated books – her first good ones, anyway – she discovered that she could form an image in her mind of where a given scene was taking place. Three-dimensional. Clear. Topographically mapped. Sometimes she could even tally up the trees in a forest or garden, without having to be told how many were there. Sometimes, she even felt herself surrounded by them, the leaf shadow dappling.

There were times as a kid when she'd put this to use. Willing the landscape on her walk to school to alter, shift: parked caravans had transformed into pumpkins or carriages; boring brown fences became tangles of thorns. She occupied her place in line outside the classroom as though it were an iron maiden, the sound of chalk on the blackboard like nails on her skin.

Sometimes, when the fighting between her parents was at its worst – when they were throwing blue and purple and bronze fireworks around the kitchen – she'd hidden even deeper in her bedroom, in her wardrobe, and when she hadn't been whisked away to Narnia, she'd shut her eyes tightly and tried to shortcut there instead.

It didn't always work.

Back then, she found it difficult to stay focused when she was that upset. She didn't have the same tools at her disposal as she does now.

She sets down her eighth glass of wine on the desk beside the mouse. It spills a little, leaves a bloody-looking ring on the pine.

She'll clean it in the morning, she tells herself.

She's busy at the minute.

Her dress swooshes as she spins on the breathless old chair.

It begins as a photograph, framed by mad Bavarian fingers.

It's out of focus at first, and colours shiver and run.

Then the fog starts to lift, and it shows clearly: the castle.

The stippled, stubbled mass of firs and pines that line the mountainside around it. Green and amber, gold and ochre in the close-to-sunset light.

Slatey-grey of rockface showing through in streaks beneath.

How to get up there?

Only a single narrow trail wends its way around the mountain. Haunted not by ghosts but by the clattering of cart-wheels, the hammering of hooves. In the rare event of a visitor approaching, those noises resound off the hillsides for days.

The castle walls seem to spring from the massif itself. As though some mammoth Michelangelo had taken up a chisel, and, with a similarly outsized mallet, split the stone clean down to this, its strange and secret core.

This peak, Donna senses, once stood almost twice as high.

Those walls ascend, all white and grey, in imitation of what they might have called back then the heavens. They stretch up and up, tapering at last, at various levels, into lance-like pinnacles of blue-rinse shale.

Donna cannot forget the tallest tower in particular, the tiny annexe that juts from just below its tip. The annexe that, to her, has always seemed so petite as to suggest it was intended for a baby. To safeguard it from threats, perhaps, or simply make it easier for fairy godmothers to reach.

She steps into the courtyard. The iron spikes of the portcullis are behind her, and ahead is a feeling of permanent spring. The courtyard is pale-stoned and bright, and topiaries, which seem like miniatures of the cliffside firs, stand at regimented intervals and ornament its borders. A flock of birds, maybe swallows, maybe swifts, scatter arrow-winged shadows on the gravel and grass.

She doesn't know for certain that the entrance hall is floored with marble.
But that's how she sees it.
She is strong-willed in matters such as this.
Interior decoration.
Internalised design.
She has a strong will and cold feet.
She wears neither jewel-laden shoes nor glass slippers. She is barefoot, here, and feels the smooth chill of the marble under her soles.

She looks down at her feet, and they don't seem too large or too weird or unwieldy.

She looks up: from the high vaulted ceiling hangs a chandelier, an inverted sculpture of the castle itself.

A wide, two-pronged stairway stretches before her. Though her naked footsteps do not echo, the brushing of her dress upon the steps behind her gives the sensation of a wave. She rides the crest to the first floor landing, turns a complete circle and marvels at the height of the hall, and at the detail of the carving in the ceiling stone and the pillars which help keep it up.

She is unable to decide which pathway to follow:

The one leading left.   Or the one leading right.

Eyes closed, she pirouettes, she spins in her chair, committed now to going where she's facing when she stops.

She hopes when that happens she isn't pointed at a wall.

Or back the way she's come.
Nowt worse than that.

Her eyelids spring open – in this fantasy only – and she's greeted by the candlelit arch to the right.

A burst of relief.

She gambols towards it, into it, onwards, leaving freeze-frame facsimiles of herself like breadcrumbs in her wake. She whirligigs down corridors, performing waltz steps with those spectres, and with her ever-present shadow, which wears its subtle shadow dress. She careers and careens and calls out her name, sends it out like a boomerang, counting the seconds it takes to come back.

Donna Creosote.

Three seconds.

Donna Creosote.

Four.

Her running takes her at last to a large double door, which opens with only the slightest of touches.
The polished silver candelabras in this chamber give out a light-level that might be best described as *mood*. The furnishings are all plush velvet, mahogany, fine laces and silks. The four-poster bed is shielded by opaque draperies, which she

thinks may be muslin, but which nonetheless remind her of the shower curtains she uses to save her bathroom books from damp.

This unwanted intrusion stirs her slightly in her chair.

Breathing deeply, she tries to regather her focus.

She steps forwards, thrills to feel the softness of the rug beneath her feet.

She looks around, absorbs the opulence of varnished wood and brand new oil paintings. There are three of the castle, from different perspectives, and one of the man she is hoping to meet.

She moves closer to the bed, brushes the curtains aside like a mist, strokes her fingers on the linen.

She crawls across the mattress, buzzing and breathless as it dips with her weight.

She lies on her back, head resting on pillows.

She doesn't make a move to unfasten her gown.

She wants to be undressed by mad Bavarian fingers.

Wants to be held by mad Bavarian hands.

Wants it so badly that, unbalanced, she tilts and then tumbles the old chair too far.

Donna sprawls on the floor beside the legs of her desk. Unhurt, or at least too drunk to feel it.

It takes her a couple of minutes to right herself, to disentangle herself from the swivel chair, and by the time she has done that, the castle is gone. Is just a double-vision photo in the distance of the screen.

There is still a glass of wine, or maybe two, beside her mouse.

After a few faulty clicks, she opens her browser.

She smiles and takes another sip.

24

Most of the vomit had fallen into the bowl.
Her hair, had it been longer, would have followed it down.

Her left ear was pressed against the horseshoe of the seat, and she could hear her blood pounding in her head like the sea in a shell. Like all of the ocean, compressed and then shaken.
No, like wind through the canopy, the rattle of leaves.
Coming to, she thought she felt something touch at her shoulder, her neck, and she jerked herself upright, but there wasn't anything there.

Apart from a mess.

Rogue chunks and liquid had spattered the floor, left and right, and splashed up at the shower curtains guarding her books.

She stood up, being careful not to step in any.
Surviving as far as the sink, the bathroom mirror, she could see the red line that arced down from just below her temple to the left side of her chin.
She rubbed at it, tenderly at first, and then roughly.
It would be a few minutes yet before it faded.

Her eyes were red, too.
Her eyelids were puffy.
Sleep was like PVA glue in the lashes.

She remembered painting that glue across her hands in art class, age six or seven. Peeling it off and setting it down on the desk like the grasp of a ghost. Or like a chrysalis, she used to think, before joining her thumbs and flapping her fingers like butterfly wings.

She let cold water trickle through them now. She cupped it in her palms and raised it, swept it up across her wine-stained lips.

Her teeth felt mossed and sweaty.
Her tongue felt similar, but denser and worse.

Squeezing toothpaste on the brush – white with a streak of gelatinous green – she felt the inevitable headache approaching. It sped up as it neared and arrived like a punch.

She remembered falling over, somewhere.

She remembered drinking far too much.

The join between her sticky teeth and her sticky gums was livid as the bristles ran against it. When she spat, there were flecks of pink wrapped up and writhing in the almost-iridescent green.
When she was finished, her mouth tasted salty, not at all like mint or minty fresh.
She would have to clean it again. Rinse and repeat.

She would have to clean up the toilet and the tiling and the bookcase, she knew, but she couldn't face it yet.

The living area, after the harsh glare of the bathroom light, was pleasingly dim. Almost pitch black, in fact, in some areas. Almost, she thought, as she stood there, leaned there, in the doorway, as though she was right back in front of that shop-window cave.

No, she thought, relying on the wall to help her edge into the kitchen: as though she was deeper in that forest, as though she had followed those breadcrumbs, those acorns, but not yet made her way back.

Had she really eaten an olive off the carpet? she wondered. Ugh. She desperately hoped she was recalling that wrong.

She couldn't remember much else, beyond that point. Arguments. Wine. The broad strokes, but no details.

She winced as her palm slapped against the front of the fridge. Colder than the rest of the wall. Rougher. A tangle of little magnetic letters on the front of it, unclear in the gloom, and she imagined them fungi, or just cracks in the bark. Couldn't help it.
The gurgle of coolant like trickling sap.
Too loud.
She swallowed.
Well, she tried, but her mouth still felt desiccated, her tongue like dried fruit.
She pushed off from the fridge and pinballed across to the coffee and mugs. The kettle, by the sink, was still half-full with water. She flicked the switch, waited, listened to it hiss.

It reminded her of her grandma: her breath, her confusion, as she got near the end.
Only sixty-three when it happened, early-onset dementia.

's'gone. She remembered.

Yes, Donna, 's'gone.

As she rooted through the cupboards looking for a clean enough mug, she noticed that the two oven trays and the pizza tray were still stacked in the sink. The places where the duct tape residue hadn't come away were covered now with a fine layer of dust.

A medium-sized pan was balanced on the strip of worktop behind the sink, between the taps. A large cheese-grater stuck up from the front of it, wonky. It looked a bit like a sculpture she remembered seeing one time. Found art, she thought was the technical term.

Though it looked kind of like a castle, too.
The silhouette of one.
That is, if she squinted, and let the headache do the rest.

Coffee steamed her forehead and her eyelids as she leaned over the cup.
She thought it might ease the aching, but it didn't really help.
Still uneasy, she picked her way across what seemed at the minute an interminable gulf, the metre-wide gap between worktop and table. Stumbling, she set her coffee down too heavily and spilled some on her fingers. Winced. Gasped.

Bastard.

She shoved the oven trays aside and ran her hand beneath the cold tap, like her parents had always told her to do. It stung – it really fucking stung – but at least it didn't seem, in this light, to be coming up in a blister.

The word *bastard* was still on her mind when she returned to her seat, drying her hand on the tea towel. She wiped the towel across the table, around the damp side of the cup. Threw it back towards the worktop.
Missed.
But she wasn't about to bend down for it now.

The word *bastard* kept circling, wouldn't leave her alone.

Even worse than the sickness, it hassled her head.

Squinting up at the fridge, in this light, she could almost swear that those letters were shifting to form it. Carved in the bark. On one side of the arrow.

She blew on her coffee, took a long sip. She could taste it better than the toothpaste, but that still wasn't much. She didn't really drink it for the flavour, though. She drank it, mostly, just to help her wake up in the morning, and then to help her stay awake and read a little more at night.

But she hadn't read a book properly for two days now.
She'd had other things to do, she thought.

Which made a change.

If she had been reading last night, she'd be a lot less fucked up today. She didn't often get too drunk when she was reading, because too much wine was guaranteed to make the words all fall apart. Let the stories get loose from behind those small black-ink bars.

There were times that was ok, of course, but she had to be careful not to get carried away.

Everything in moderation, her Grandma used to tell her.

Except love, Donna. You can never get enough of that. A sly little wink. A sly little laugh.

Used to tell her that it was important to have lots of friends. *Make the most of them while you're young, because they won't be around for long after.*

Her Christmas card list, she said once, had shrunk to the size of a joke from a cracker.

The few occasions when Donna talked online to friends these days, she liked to have a drink beside her. Drinking filled the gaps between responses.

Drinking took her back to how it used to be when they'd met up in the park.

Sometimes she didn't even buy red wine to drink, just cheap imported beer and bargain-brand cider.

Sometimes she just drank and surfed the internet for stupid shit and cat photos that didn't make her laugh.

She might have been doing that last night, she thought.

She'd clearly been too rat-arsed to do much of owt else.

She checked over her shoulder, squinting in the dimness towards the open laptop. It was darker still than the surroundings, but the blue LED above the keyboard was flashing, letting her know that she hadn't shut it down before bed.

Or rather, before bathroom.

Skin prickling, Donna shuffled towards the pull of that light, that will o' the wisp, taking care not to trip over the beanbag en route. Balancing her coffee with an egg and spoon grace, barely, she told herself, spilling a drop.

Reaching the desk, she pushed the button to wake the machine. Slumped down in the chair. As she waited, she noticed the ring of red wine beneath last night's glass.

The list of things she had to clean kept growing and growing.

It seemed she'd sent Sammy a message last night.

You wanna come over? x

Was all that it said.

25

Hi, sorry I didn't reply last night, had to get an early night because I'm working. I'm on my lunch break now, are you ok.. do you still want me to come over? x

He had replied.

With a kiss.

Bastard.

She said it half to him and half to herself.

Maybe even sixty-forty. Weighted heavier to her.

She always did this.
That is, she had always done this in the past.
Got lonely, got drunk, sent out a random invitation. Either in person or by text, or by email, or by just plain phoning up. Invariably hearing *Please leave your message after the tone*, and not even considering doing anything but. Going on for a minute, sometimes, about how she thought the guy in question was a good guy and *I like talking to you and do you want to spend time together? I want to spend time with you because you're a good guy* and on and on until the message service cut her off.

That was how things had happened with Kirk.

Donna Crick-Oakley had called him after she'd been up late swilling cider, probably a week after first meeting him and not being impressed. She'd told him she thought he was a hottie, and asked him, in her broadest Yorkshire accent, did he *want to 'ave some fun?*

This had been at half-two in the morning, and so it wasn't perhaps surprising it had gone through to answerphone, and Kirk hadn't got back in touch with her until half-eight the morning after, just before he left for work.

He hadn't phoned her, though. He'd texted.

> *Donna :) hows you this morning? Wish i hadn't been asleep last night!! I think you're a hottie too girl! Wanna meet later :)*

At least, she thought, he hadn't put a kiss.

Thinking back now, though, two smiley faces seemed a grim foreshadowing of what was to come. Always over-eager, always too excited about playing with a certain part of his toy to stop and consider that his toy might have things beyond that playing on its mind.

And another thing about Kirk was that he texted her too much. Sent her texts like that first one, sent her texts asking how she was doing, all of the time.

Donna, for all that she liked reading, did not like reading texts.

The boyfriend before Kirk, he hadn't texted much at all.
Which had been good.
At first.
But then, on a whim one morning, she had checked his phone and found that he'd been sending all his texts to someone else.

Bitch.

The other three, they hadn't really been relationships, she guessed. There'd been a few dates and a few fucks with each of them, but not much more than that.

One of them had been a part of the group who hung out in the park, though, and that was kind of why she'd stopped going.

He hadn't taken her saying *not again* to him too well.

Still, she always did this.

And, given the message on her screen, it seemed she wasn't about to stop.

Was a guy like Sammy really right for her, though, for what she was wanting?

Did she know what she was wanting?

She knew what she'd been wanting last night. At least, she could guess.

And she was prepared to admit to herself she was lonely.

But she didn't want anything *serious*.

And the reply that Sammy had sent seemed hesitant, apologetic, even. Not something that she wanted. Even worse for her, from past experience, than being over-eager.

But maybe that hesitance was his try at being respectful. Maybe that meant he was closer to being manly than any of the others. That he'd treat her fairly and fuck her right.

Maybe it meant he was lonely too, and horny too, but just like herself didn't want to be hurt.

Yes, that would be nice, she typed. How about half 7?

Then, thinking on, she sent: Please bring some wine :) x

26

Donna pushed the vacuum cleaner around the carpet by the beanbag, resisting the nagging temptation to dance. To spin the long-handled machine around on its pivot, rehearsing, perhaps, some moves for tonight.

It wasn't too difficult to hold back, in the end, given how skewwhiff her tummy still felt. Which had been made worse again by having to deal with the mess in the bathroom, and wasn't exactly being helped by the creeping aroma of bleach.

Indeed, it was quite likely that on any other day she'd have already gone back to bed. Maybe taken a book with her, for comfort, but probably not. Just curled up beneath the covers, in her pyjamas, embracing the warmth for a change as she sweated it out.

No simpler detox.

But she hadn't really left herself that option here. She could still cancel, of course, or perhaps try and postpone until tomorrow. Though that wasn't exactly the best way to start. And it would depend on a lie, because she couldn't give him the actual reason: a lass who got that drunk on her own wasn't likely to appeal.

Neither was a lass who lived in her own filth.

Going at the bottom of the bookcase with the brush attachment, she sucked up the remaining two olives she hadn't salvaged last night. They rattled in the chamber and then stopped, as if pulped. She swept the brush across the spines, the dust jackets, surprised at how rough they still looked when she'd done. A couple of times she heard a noise like a twig snapping, but when she looked inside she couldn't see any signs. Just a tangle of thread. She carried on up the shelves.

Donna moved the empty bottles into the store cupboard along with the rest. She should probably take them out to recycle at some point, but the longer she left it the more of a problem it was. Didn't have time to make several trips to the ground floor at the moment, and besides, it wasn't as if she'd have cause to go in there tonight.

The sink, on the other hand, could scarce be avoided: the pan and the oven trays were still lingering there. She set on with the scouring pad to try remove all the gunk, even using some old rubber gloves so it didn't just transfer to her hands. There was far too much foam, though, and the bubbles went everywhere, floating up by her face; one even popped in her eye.

She remembered that at some point she'd thought bubbles were fairies, that they held fairies, that it was cruel and unusual to force them to clean.

On the last point at least, her thoughts hadn't altered.

Leaving the cookware to soak, fighting the urge to say *sod it* and just go for a nap, she made herself crack on with clearing up the cupboards, and then she straightened the letters on the door of the fridge. She toyed with the idea of putting them in alphabetical order, but thought that might be taking it a little too far. This was, after all, about being as un-weird as possible.

Besides, that would probably take quite a while, given how there were several of each letter, and it was already getting on for quarter past four. She wanted to leave enough time to get herself sorted.

To shower.

To shave her legs.

To find the right necklace to go with her dress.

She lifted her jewellery box out of the second drawer in her bedside table, and set it down on her lap. There was a tiny ballerina on top who was supposed to pirouette a few times if you pressed a small button, though the mechanism had jammed years ago and all she did nowadays was tremble a little, as though she had stage fright or was going into shock. The music no longer played when Donna opened the lid.

She'd been meaning to get a new one for ages, but she didn't really take it out that often and so the thought had kept slipping her mind. She tended to think how many books she could get for the price of those earrings, or the cost of that bracelet, and so rarely added anything to the collection inside.

Not that her mother gave her any credit for that budgeting strategy.

At any rate, the box wasn't as old as some of the trinkets it carried, most of them either being gifts from as far back as her christening, or else handed down after her grandma had died.

She held up a couple of silver chains to the glare from the bulb, trying to work out which of them caught the light better. Which of them sparkled as much as she thought a princess' should.

The one with the amethyst, she decided. White gold drizzled round it like honey or milk.

Fixing it around her neck, she turned to examine herself in the mirror. But it wasn't the gem that caught her eye so much as the dried-in island of vomit at the bottom of her dress.

Shit!

How had she not seen it earlier?

What in the actual fuck was she going to do now?

She could hardly wear her hoody or her boob-tube again. And a sluttier dress might send the wrong message.

Back in the kitchen, she held the gown on the table, rubbing at the stain with a washing-up cloth. The pallid chunks came away but the wet patch the work left was the size of a hardback. And small flecks of adhesive seemed to have been carried across.

Donna stood on her balcony, letting the dress blow in the breeze like an oversized handkerchief, her royal favour, as though she were trying to attract the attention of yet more comely suitors. As though she'd soon have so many she could start turning them down.

As though she could afford to call off tonight and get a good sleep, safe in the knowledge there'd be more interest tomorrow.

But down below on the pavement nobody stopped to look up.

27

Everybody is searching for their true love, their future girlfriend or boyfriend or husband or wife.

The world according to some of the books in Donna Creosote's flat.

Nobody keeps them.
The world according to Donna Crick-Oakley's experience.

It is a kind of bravery to wait behind the door and expect wine or roses when it opens.

Donna let that thought run across her mind as she stood there, at twenty-six minutes past seven, wearing an old silvery silk-effect top and her last surviving pair of skinny jeans. She'd have to take the dress to the dry-cleaners tomorrow.

She had already seen Sammy approaching the building.

She'd been watching from the balcony.

Tonight, there were no fireworks rising from the lower floors. No parties either. Not yet.

Still, early doors, as her father used to say.

Thinking of her father before she met a date was an odd constant in her life. Odd not necessarily because he was her father, but because he hadn't been in her life when she'd had any dates. Any serious ones, anyway.

She didn't count being taken out for her prom.
It hadn't ended well.

Though perhaps in that case she should really include it.
It certainly fit the trend.

It is another kind of armour, isn't it, to have such cynicism at the start?

But, she wondered, after what she'd been through the other day, did she really need more armour?

Did she want it?

Would it matter, anyway, once she'd had a drink or two? Or three?

The knock came.
Loud enough, but a little hesitant. The pause between the second tap and the third had been slightly too long to have been an intended skipped beat.

Donna took her time to reach for the handle.
Thirty seconds, or thereabouts.
Making him wait.

Hi there.

Hello.

Good to – How are you?

Good, thanks. And you?

Good. Thank you. Good. How about –

How about what?

No, sorry, I was just going to ask how you were again.

Oh, ok.

Sorry, I think I'm still recovering. The lift isn't working, so I had to take the stairs.

Oh, you're kidding! Really?

Yeah.

So you had to walk up all twelve flights?

Is that how many? Shit – I mean, sorry for that – just catching my breath.

It's ok, Sam. We're both adults here.

Yeah, guess we are. And, it's Sammy. Sorry.

Ok.

Ok. I've got this for you, by the way.

He pulled a plastic bag from out behind his back, and withdrew a bottle from inside it.

Almost a magic trick.

It was rosé, though. Donna didn't much care for rosé. Especially not sparkling.

Still, she smiled and took it.

The story of her life.

Thank you. That's very kind, but you didn't have to.

You asked, so I thought I would.

He smiled.

She smiled back.

She hadn't exactly *asked*.

Well, thanks. Would you like a glass now?

Do you have any beer? If that's ok?

I don't have any in at the moment. Sorry. If you don't fancy wine, I can just save it?

No. No, don't be daft. I'll have a glass with you.

Ok, good.

Because Donna wasn't about to drink a whole bottle of rosé by herself.
Not when she wasn't alone.

Come in, then. I'll just get the glasses.

Ok.

If you want to sit at the table, just go ahead.

Ok.

I did have a couch, but it was old, so I gave it to charity. I'm just waiting to find a good deal on another, actually.

She used to have an extra beanbag.

Yeah, I know the feeling.

Really?

Yeah. I've just moved out from my parents', and I'm still looking for furniture. My Dad said he'd drive me to Ikea, but he hasn't done yet. Been busy, you know?

Yeah. Don't you drive, then?

Well, I do drive. I've got a license and everything. But I don't have a car at the moment, because of the move and everything I can't really afford it. With petrol going up all the time and whatnot.

You say 'whatnot'?

Did I? Sorry –

Stop apologising. I just meant that it sounds kinda...posh.

Does it?

Not 'posh' posh, maybe, but kinda like something a Southerner might say. It's a bit cut glass. Queen's English, you know?

Really?

Yeah, go on. Say it, like, all Southern, and you'll see what I mean.

What? 'Whatnot'? But surely if you say anything all Southern it's going to sound... Southern.

Well, he had her there.

She laughed at herself, a little, and pushed a large glass of wine across the table. Watched the way he held it like a beer glass, with his hand around the body, rather than the stem.
She'd do the same now.

So, how did work go? Was that pie-in-demand thing starting today, or is that at the weekend?

That's at the weekend. And it's pie-on-demand. But we did take a few orders. Five, I think.

That's good.

Yeah. Are you sure you don't want one?

No. I mean, yes, I'm sure. But thank you.

Ok. If you change your mind –

Ok, thanks.

Donna drank her wine. Didn't exactly savour it, just swallowed it down.

Have you been up to much?

Not much since yesterday, no.

Certainly not getting hammered and fantasizing about a long-dead Bavarian king.

Oh, ok.

Ok.

So, you haven't heard from any of the others or anything?

Since yesterday? No. Did you send that message out yet? I mean, I didn't get it, so probably not. Right?

Yeah.

What, you did, or you didn't?

Didn't.

Ok.

She watched him gulp at his wine, glance around at the flat.

She couldn't tell whether he appreciated the tidiness or not.

You don't have a TV?

No. Unfortunately –

It's ok, I understand. I don't either.

What, you don't like to watch it? Or you just don't have one?

Oh. I do like to watch it, I guess. You know, sometimes. I don't really like British TV, you know. All the cop shows are shit – sorry – and I don't like soaps or anything. Just fuc– just stupid plots and an excuse for rape and murder everywhere.

Sounds like a Viking invasion.

That's exactly what I said when Jim's wife was telling me earlier. And all she said to that is, 'Weren't they in York?' Man, I swear, if she wrote soaps they'd be much better. She's like my Mum, only even more batshit, and I don't have to pretend that she makes any sense, you know?

Doesn't Jim mind you laughing at his wife, though?

Nah, he's all for it. It's all good-natured, you know? She's sweet, really. Just a bit out of her tree. She's twelve years older than him, and he's getting on a bit, so I guess it's a bit of the old, erm...

Senile dementia?

Yeah, that'd be it. Bit odd to forget, isnit?

Yeah.

> She didn't like the way he said *isnit*.

> She poured herself another glass of wine.

> Didn't offer him a top-up.

> He didn't seem to notice.

American TV's alright, though. It's much better. Especially the cop shows. I think they get bigger budgets, but it's also just better quality. When they can afford to have that many episodes in a season, they're really under pressure to deliver good stories, you know?

Yeah.

And US sitcoms are much better as well. Much funnier. And the chicks in them are –

Are what?

I was going to say they're – always hotter. I'm sorry. I didn't mean you're not, or anything –

It's ok. Don't worry about it.

　　She let the half-compliment go. If he thought it, she wanted him to say it outright.

How come you don't have a TV, though? If you like all those shows.

Oh, yeah. I just haven't bought one yet. I had to get a cooker and a fridge and things. You know, the essentials. Lucky for me I work for Jim, because he was able to get me a fridge for really cheap. And it's a fairly new one, too. He used to have it in his shed, before he moved house himself in January. They're closer to the hospital now.

Oh, ok. That makes sense, I guess.

How about you? Are you waiting to find one, or what?

A TV?

Yeah.

No.

How come? Just use your computer?

Don't really watch it.

You don't like it? You ever seen CSI?

No, never.

What about the sitcoms?

Not really. I watched some of *Friends* back in the day, but my mum didn't like it, so we didn't watch much. It was good, though. What I saw.

Sammy topped his glass up, offered more to her.

She nodded yes.

Lots of bookcases, you've got. Lots of books.

Yeah.

That's cool. What sort are they?

Just books, I suppose. You know, kinda girly ones.

That's not very descriptive, for someone who reads a lot.

I know, it wasn't really, was it?

If a customer came up to me and said, 'So, what sort of pies do you have?' and I said, 'You know, kinda fishy ones,' I'd probably get fired.

So, what, you're going to fire me?

Maybe.

Really?

Don't be fucking daft.

What?

Daft, I meant. Don't be daft. Sorry.

I'm just messing with you. You can swear, you know. I've heard bad words before.

She wondered if he was thinking *I'll bet you have*, but somehow managing to hold his tongue.

C'mon, then. What sort of girly books? Don't think you've escaped the question so easy.

Well, they're not all girly. Just some are a bit more girly than others.

I might have to rethink that firing decision.

He paused, sipping slowly at his wine.

Donna didn't know how he could take his time with it like that. It tasted like fizzy vinegar.

Well, that would be a shame.

It would. So are you gonna tell me?

Just really girly books. You wouldn't like them. There's no cops or Americans or anything in them.

So, we're talking, like, Mills & Boon stuff here?

No. No, we are not.

She knew that most of those weren't really that dirty, but still felt herself blushing.

Really? You're going red.

And he'd noticed.

Which was exactly why people wore armour.

I bet it's all high-end 'erotica', isn't it? Daring move, putting it in your living room –

It's not. It's really not –

You're still blushing. I don't believe you. I bet it's all Northern an' all, isn't it? Fifty Shades of Gravy, and T' Story of Ooah?

Sammy was laughing as he stood up and moved towards the shelves.

As she rose to follow him, she noticed that he was a good few inches taller than her, and also that the swagger he'd been showing off the day before had all but disappeared.

He reached the bookcase before she'd properly left her seat, pulled out a book and started scanning the back cover.

Oh, so it's like fairytales and fantasy and things? That's cool. That's good stuff.

He almost sounded disappointed.

Really? Do you like them?

Well, I'm not really into the fairy stories, like Cinderella and things. I like The Lion King, and Toy Story, I guess, but that's about as far as I got with Disney.

Yeah, me too.

I do like some fantasy stories, though.

Yeah?

Yeah, like, ones with all the swords and –

Hot chicks?

I was going to say 'whatnot'. But, yeah, mainly. Conan, and all that. Lots of things that are pretty much Conan but with different names. And I used to have tons, well, a few, of these big books on myths, you know, which were really cool. Do you know what I'm on about? Those big, they're probably bigger than A4, books, with little stories from Greek and Norse myth, and with those really great pictures in. I had one of the Odyssey that I swear I read like twenty times in the first week I got it.

Really? Yeah, I know the ones you mean. They're awesome.

Yeah. Really awesome. I used to sleep with them under my pillow. Whichever one I was reading at the time.

Oh.

Is that weird? Does that make me sound weird? The way you said that then, it sounds as if you think that's weird.

No. Not weird. It's just, I didn't expect you to say it. I mean, I know where you're coming from. I've done similar stuff.

Like slept with storybooks under your pillow?

Well –

Really? You have, haven't you? Do you still do it?

It's not that I – no, I don't sleep with them under my pillow.

What is it then?

Nothing.

Aww, c'mon. Tell me.

No.

I won't tell anyone. Promise. Look, wine-promise.

    He took a sip.

What the hell's a 'wine-promise'? Sounds Southern to me.

It's where I promise, and then I drink wine to seal the deal. See?

    He took another.

Oh.

That one meant I'm weird, didn't it?

Yes.

You must be weird too, though, if you won't tell me what you do with your books. Do you have a fort in your bedroom? You have a fucking fort in your bedroom, don't you?

No. Stop guessing.

No. Do you, erm, sleep under a blanket made of books? Like, all sewn together and whatnot?

No. You won't guess.

I will. Do you keep books inside your teddy bears?

No. You're being stupid. Look, just hold on.

She turned and moved towards the bedroom.

She heard him start to follow.

Just wait here, ok. You're not going to see it tonight.

Oh.

She turned again and left him there.

When she came back, she was carrying a book.

Is that what I think it is?

Yep.

You've actually got it?

Yep.

She handed it over, watching his face. His eyes especially, and his mouth.

She liked his smile.

She wouldn't kiss it tonight, though.
She'd make him wait until the second date for that.

28

A re they ready yet?

Donna had asked Sammy to pick up some cheese on his way over.

He'd arrived saying that he hadn't been sure what sort of cheese to get.

Before he left last night, she'd let him know, for future reference, that she didn't really like rosé. He'd apologised for guessing wrong.

Then he'd said: *Would you like to try rose B?*

He'd brought a couple of four-cheese pizzas instead, he told her, in a bid to cover as many bases as he could.

He'd also brought a bottle of red.

He called over to her from the desk. She was in the kitchen, fixing drinks. They'd set up the dining chairs in front of the computer, so that they could watch old sitcom episodes they found online.

You have to see this, he'd said.

Not quite. Depends how done you want them?

What?

131

How crispy do you want them?

I'm easy. Whatever you want.

I prefer them crispy.

That's cool.

I'll give them another few minutes.

Ok. Come look at this.

    He showed her a clip from *Friends*. She remembered it. Must have been from an episode she'd seen.
    She still laughed, though.

And this one. This is cool, gets me every time. Just wait for it.

    She laughed, and she watched him laughing.

    They moved back to the kitchen to eat, because Donna didn't want to get any crumbs or stains on the carpet.

I won't spill. Promise, he'd said.

I will, she'd said. Wine-promise.

    She took a sip of the red that he'd bought. It didn't taste like vinegar, which was always a good start.

    Sammy smiled.

Thanks for letting me take that book home, by the way.

No worries. Did you read it, then?

I know we've probably gone beyond this point already, but would it make me sound, I dunno, childish, if I said yes?

Which point did he mean?

Oh, incredibly. But, like you say, I'd already come to that conclusion.

Ok. In that case, I read the hell out of it.

Really?

Really, yeah. I even tried to read it how I read it, well, how I read my copy, back in the day. See if...

'See it' what?

You know, if it kinda made me feel younger or whatnot. If it really brought me back to how things were when I was a kid.

And did it?

Not really.

Oh. That's a shame.

Yeah.

How did you used to read it, though? Just out of curiosity.

She drank more wine. Took a bite of her pizza.

She wasn't sure that she could really taste four distinct types of cheese.

And don't say naked, or while standing on your head.

Why not?

Because I won't believe you.

Why not?

Because I happen to have conducted extensive research into both methods, and the results have not been promising.

For reading, you mean?

Yes.

Interesting. Although, you clearly haven't tried them both at the same time.

Oh. And you have, I suppose?

He nodded, grinning.

Care to state your findings?

I'm afraid that information's classified.

Really? That's not very fair.

Fair's got nowt to do with it. It's on a need to know basis.

And I don't need to know?

We'll see.

He finished his glass of wine and took a bite from a slice of pizza.

Smooth bastard.

Ok. Well, what if I tell you a secret first? Would that get me clearance?

He took another bite of pizza. Refilled his glass. Refilled hers.

It might. It depends what the secret is though, doesn't it?

You're mean.

I'm sorry. But you still have to tell me a secret.

Do you promise you'll tell me once I've told you?

Ok then.

Say it.

I promise.

Good. Now, wine-promise.

You're trying to get me drunk, aren't you?

Maybe.

Don't change the subject. Wine-promise.

Ok, I wine-promise.

He sipped. Ate more pizza.

Ok. So, my secret is –

I'm listening.

Ok. Ok. Well, my secret is, I used to hate you.

Oh. Right. Now who's mean?

Well, there it is. Now you've got to tell me yours.

Hang on a minute, lass. You've just said you used to hate me. Now, that's not very nice, but neither is it very secret. You were a girl – of course you hated me. In fact, every girl used to hate me. All through secondary school. That was, like, the defining factor of my life.

Well, I didn't go to the same secondary school, so I didn't know. So, my secret still stands.

Nope. Nope, nope, nope. Them's not the rules. You either tell me another secret – preferably something naughty – or you fill out the details on the one you've already said.

Really not fair. But, I suppose, because I'm nice, I'll tell you.

Go on, then.

Ok. Well, here goes.

I'm listening.

Well, when I said I used to hate you, what I meant is that I used to tell people I hated you. I told the teachers, my parents, my friends. I even told myself. But the only reason I did that, I think, is because –

Because?

Because I had a little, a very, very tiny — like, teensy weensy — crush. On you.

Interesting. Very interesting.

> He made a show of stroking the faint stubble on his chin.
> It still suited him.
> The bastard.

Now, it's your turn.

Hold on. I'm wondering about something. I need time to wonder.

What is there to wonder about? I've just told you my secret, now it's your turn. Tell me about your reading practices. I demand to know.

> She banged on the table with pantomime exaggeration, shaking their glasses.

Ok, ok. Hold your horses. I'm just wondering, since I can tell you're really dying to know, if it was the same thing in secondary school. You know, people, girls acting like they hated me, but actually crushing on me realllly bad. Because, if so, then it turns out I was a stud.

> He grinned at her again. Bits of herb and flecks of pizza crust were still between his teeth.
> She didn't point them out.

Ok, I think you're done wondering. Now, spill.

I thought you didn't want any spilling. Thought that's why we're at the table?

Aww, c'mon, I told you mine. And it was a big one.

Yeah, suppose.

'Suppose'?

Ok. Ok, I'll tell you.

Chop, chop.

Ok. Well, I used to read my books at home in my bedroom, right? Like most kids.

Do they read any more?

I dunno. My cousins don't, but my parents aren't talking to their parents at the minute, so... not really my problem.

Oh. Sorry.

It's ok.

Good. Now, back to it.

Ok. Don't rush me. I used to read in my bedroom, but because I wasn't allowed to put my light on during the day because it wasted electric, and because I shared a bunk bed with my brother and he had the top bunk, so I was stuck underneath it, I had to find some way to get better reading light.

Ok.

I couldn't just go up onto my brother's bunk, you know, because if he caught me up there, I'd get beats. So, anyway, I ended up sitting on the windowsill. I used to sit there with my book open across my knees, and I'd alternate between reading and staring out of my window at whatever, you know. And it was really good, really calming to do.

So, how come it didn't work when you tried it last night?

Well, turns out my arse is much bigger than it used to be. I tried getting up on the windowsill at my new place, and I sort of got balanced but then I fell off.

Donna Creosote laughed and nearly shot wine through her nose.

She swallowed, composed herself.

That's kinda sweet, you know, in a stupid sorta way.

Well, thanks.

But I thought you were going to tell me all you know about being naked when you're standing on your head.

29

It had cost her a little extra, but Donna had managed to have the dry cleaners get her dress back to her within twenty-four hours.

Just in time for Sammy's third visit.

She'd let things happen before on the first night, and she'd made a couple of her lovers wait it out until the fourth.

She'd shaved her legs again this morning, and contemplated once more what to do with her pubis. She didn't think, all things considered, that it was the hair a proper fairy tale princess should let grow too long.

She tried not to pay too much attention to the stretchmarks above her hips, or to the jut of those hips, or the higher-up jut of her collarbone. Tried hard not to look at those places too much, as she put on her underwear and shimmied into her gown.

She did her makeup.

She re-did it. Twice.

She pinned her hair up, then let it fall free, then tied it back in a loose bun.

She liked the feeling that came with letting it down again later.

She remembered liking that feeling.

The amethyst necklace went well. Looked fine, as she stood on the floor of books and stared more at her dress than at herself.

Looked good, even.

Great.

In the message she'd sent him earlier, she'd asked not only that he bring another bottle of wine, but that he dress up smart as well. Watching herself twirl in the mirror, she hoped that he'd taken the hint.

When he arrived, he sort of had and sort of hadn't.

He was wearing jeans again, but he had on a shirt – a nice, neat black one – and had trimmed his stubble. Which was good, because it had rubbed a little at her cheeks and chin and neck the night before.

Not that she'd minded too much, she supposed.

They sat across the small dining table again, and Donna poured the wine. First to him, then to herself. They clinked glasses and drank, and Donna hoped the lip gloss she'd put on would stop the wine from staining.

They kissed, gently; partly, on Donna's side, so that she didn't lose that shine too soon.

I sent that message out to everyone earlier. Did you see?

Yeah. Thanks for including me. This time.

I'm sorry about last time. Won't happen again, lass.

It'd better not.

Ok.

Just messin'. Has anyone replied yet?

Not yet, no.

Well, hopefully they will do soon. It'd be good to see them again, maybe go and have a proper night out, you know. It's been ages since I had one of them.

Yeah, I know what you mean. Jim's not really one for clubbing.

What about his wife?

I dunno. She might be up for it. Sure you wouldn't get jealous, though?

No, go ahead.

I'll ask her on Saturday, then.

That's tomorrow.

Is it?

Yep.

Really? Shit.

What time do you start?

About half-seven, I'm on. But it'll be fine.

You should have said, we could have rearranged it. Rescheduled for tomorrow night or something.

Yeah, we could've. But it'll be fine.

You sure?

Of course. Besides, I kinda wanted to see you tonight.

Oh, really?

Maybe.

She sipped her wine, smiling.

You're blushing again, lass.

Am not.

Totally are.

He stuck out his tongue.

It was a kind of grapey purple.

And I know how to make it worse.

No you don't, because I'm not blushing. See?

She did her best to cool her face down, hold it steady.

It didn't work.

I used to have a crush on you as well.

Really? You're just saying that.

I'm not. You know on the really cold nights out at the park, when everyone was trying to keep their hands warm with fag lighters

143

and talking about how it probably wouldn't be a problem if we started a campfire?

Yeah –

Well, the only reason I came outside on those nights was to see you.

Now, you really are just saying that.

It's true. Honest. 'Cause I always had bad circulation in my hands and my feet, and that kind of cold, the bloody cold we get round here most of the time, it goes right through me. And I've never found a pair of gloves or boots that really does the trick, you know?

Ok, I believe you. I think.

Good, you should.

But was it only then? I mean, during college and whatnot?

How do you mean, 'and whatnot', Southerner?

He grinned.

She tried not to.

I mean, did you fancy me before then?

Well, I didn't know you in secondary school, and I don't think I really knew much about girls before then, so...

Oh, ok.

But I'm sure I would've done, if I had. If I'd known.

I always thought you maybe did in primary school. I bet you don't remember, do you, but you used to call me Donna Creosote. You used to pull my hair and push me into walls and get me done and call me that.

Donna Creosote? Really, did I? That's well harsh.

Well, it's a bit weird, more than harsh, probably.

I'm sorry, anyway. I'm taking it you didn't like being called that?

Not really. But mainly because I didn't know what it meant, I think.

Yeah, I used to forget the other kids' dads didn't paint fences, and didn't get to ride around on those big petrol mowers. It was just, you know when you're brought up around something, when you spend so much time with things being one way –

And it's hard to think about other people doing it differently. Yeah, I know.

Yeah.

But, just so you know, I don't hate the name now. I kind of, like you said, I got used to it. You called me it so many times, and I spent so much time thinking about it, that it stuck, I suppose. It grew on me.

In, like, a good way?

Yeah. I think so. I mean, you know how my dad went away, right?

Yeah, you did tell me. Sorry.

It's ok, it's not as if it's your fault. Before then, anyway, before the divorce and the moving out and everything, they used to fight all the time, like proper fucking shouting matches that probably the whole street could hear. It wasn't as if they meant for it to affect me, to hurt me, but there's no way you can be in the middle of all that and not get hurt. You know?

Definitely.

And well, the worse this got, the more it went on, the more I started to really not like them. It wasn't just that I didn't like being in the house with them, but that I didn't like them as people. I couldn't wait to be old enough to move out and become my own legal guardian and to change my name. And the only other name, the only alternative I could think of was what you'd called me, was Donna Creosote. Cause I didn't want to give up the Donna bit, and get rid of it entirely.

Oh.

And I thought so long and so hard about all that, about actually going through with the whole deed poll procedure, just getting my name changed and then starting a new life, and that name really helped me.

Well, I'm glad, I guess. Not for all you went through, though. I mean, that all sounds shitty –

It was.

But, you didn't change your name in the end, then? I mean, it doesn't show up that you have done online.

No, I didn't. I forgot about it in the end, I think. And with spending all that time in the courtroom with my dad and mum, I just don't think I could handle anything even remotely to do with the law.

That's understandable.

And I just didn't see that changing it would make it any better, back then. I didn't want my dad to be happy, is what it was. I didn't want to believe that fucking off and leaving us and leaving here could make him happy. And because I didn't want to believe that of him, I couldn't believe it of myself.

So, that's when you started reading?

What makes you say that?

Well, there's got to be some reason for it. For all these books, I mean.

What's wrong with having all these books? You make it sound like it's a problem.

I'm sorry, sorry. I didn't mean to. I didn't mean it that way.

Well, how did you mean it?

I just meant that, I meant that there's a lot of time here, on your shelves. It must have taken a few years to read through them all, I'm guessing. So I just figured that you started reading around then.

Oh. Right.

I'm sorry, I didn't mean to upset you. I know you don't like talking about all this stuff.

She dabbed the back of her thumbs against the corners of her eyes. Checking them afterwards to make sure they weren't smudged with mascara.

Are you ok?

She didn't respond. She was holding her right thumb and forefinger over her eyelids.

Donna? Are you ok?

He got up and walked around the table, set his hands upon her shoulders.

Would it help if I called you Miss Creosote from now on?

I don't think so, I'm sorry...

Oh.

I'm sorry, Sammy. It's not you. It's not your fault. It's just...

It's ok. C'mon, lass, calm down. It's ok.

Ok.

And I didn't mean to overreact, when you said about the books. I'm not usually like that.

I'm really not.

Wine-promise?

I think I've probably had enough wine for the night.

Ok.

I'll regular promise, though.

Go on then.

I promise that I'm not usually like that. And I'm sorry again. I mean, I do have a lot of books. A *lot*. So I shouldn't have snapped. This isn't even most of them.

I know. I've been in the bathroom.

Oh, shit, yeah.

It's ok. It's cool, actually. When you're used to a lad's mag, and toilet roll with 'knock, knock' jokes on it, you appreciate the variety.

Donna smiled.

She was ready, she thought, to let him see her bedroom floor.

30

S ammy had wanted to stay in bed longer, but he couldn't.

He hadn't wanted to turn up late for work.

Donna had tried not to pester him. Too much.
She understood.

Honestly, I do. It's ok.

She tried not to miss his warmth beside her. Tried not to miss the pressing of his cock against the small of her back as they spooned.

After showering, she noticed that he'd left a cartoon heart to show up in the condensation on the mirror.

Soft bastard.
She smiled.

Drew an arrow through it.

Then paused.

She moved the curtain from the bookcase by the toilet, closed her eyes and trailed her fingers over its contents like Braille. Like the thick strands of bark that knotted all together to make the tallest, biggest trees. The Major Oak in Sherwood. The Snow Queen's vast parliament of Norwegian pines.

She could do with being somewhere like that now, she thought, darting like a wild thing from one to the next. Like Wart as a squirrel. Young Arthur. Or as an ant, or a falcon. Anything primal like that, just to keep her mind busy. Or, rather, to let such things busy themselves in her mind, while she took a break.

Because she overthought everything, on mornings after nights like that.

And, in overthinking, she'd fucked things up before.

Still, at the first mention of a prince in this story, she couldn't help how her mind shifted to something brand new.

To the first time.
And the second.
And the third.
And the chance of more to come.

To the future. To all the things the future might bring.
Not just sex, and company, but houses. Children. Family.

She'd not been wanting anything serious. Not been wanting to think of futures such as that, of futures including that other f-word, the one she didn't like to hear.

She might not be again, once the buzz had faded – however long that took – but for now, sitting on the toilet, naked except for the book spread out across her lap, *serious* was all.

Reading, keeping her eyes trained not on the distance but on the nearer-in horizon lines of text, Donna Crick-Oakley wanted to skim to the end. To the *happily ever after* she knew that this book closed with.

That dot, the full-stop that rounded off the final sentence; that was what she wanted. It was only a little speck of ink but it could cover any holes. Any gaps, any faults, any outlying data that didn't fit the chosen trend.

That's what *happily ever after* was, she thought. A way to fudge the results, to make sure that the outcome you wanted had the highest probability. That it occupied the peak of the bell-curve on the graph.

It was the most fantastical thing about any such story.
The biggest lie.

She wanted to believe it, but it was difficult today.

She couldn't stop thinking about statistics now, about bell-curves, about how their defining aesthetic feature was their symmetry, was that they ended at the same level as they began. On the same plateau: an x axis that, as Donna thought of it, was always set at nought.

In fairy tales, the only common state that runs contrary to that – the only plateau raised higher than zero – is found in *Sleeping Beauty*. The main part of the story, as Donna knows it, takes place while the eponymous Beauty is asleep. While she's trapped in a deep and seemingly unshakeable slumber for one hundred years.

Whilst she cannot talk to anybody in the world during this time, nor inherit her kingdom, neither can she age. Her defining feature, beauty, does not desert her as she lays there, comatose and beyond the help of any save her one true love.

Yet once her true love finds her, and wakes her with the miracle of his kiss, she is welcomed back to time, to consciousness. She is exposed to the ravages of entropy, against her will – because how can anybody resent dreaming for a hundred years or more?

With a kiss, she is re-birthed into a world in which the two things that have constituted her character, her way of being – that is, her sleeping and her beauty – are already either stripped from her, or soon to be diminished.

Such was the purity of the state that had sustained her for a century, so perfectly was she shielded from decay, that no amount of *happily ever afters* could give her sanctuary now.

In comparison, that standard fairy tale get-out-of-jail-free card pales.

It's only a kiss, but it puts her life back in motion.

It may set the bell-curve to rising for a little while, but there will come a point, probably soon, at which the only way is down.

Even kisses at the end of messages were now, for Donna, an indication of where that downward turn would lead.

x marks not the spot but the axis.

To Donna Crick-Oakley's mind, right now, that axis was the line her father drew when he chose to disappear.

And that's the thing now. Even though her father hasn't properly been around since she started dating, he's a constant in her head.

Not at *certain* times.
But after them.
Around them.

Drinking helped to block him out. Helped to stop her overthinking. Books alone were not enough. Reading was something that she got from him, was a hand-me-down, almost as much of a genetic trait as her hair. Reading was part of her.

She couldn't stop. She didn't want to. But at times like this books weren't enough.

Not by themselves.

When she did it right, this mixing gave to Donna Creosote what Sleeping Beauty had, but better.

She, at least, could dance around whilst she was blacked-out to the world.

31

The red wine on Donna's lips is beautiful. She isn't looking in a mirror, but she's as certain as she gets. Anything about her can be beautiful today.

She can even dress herself in foil and duct tape, if she wants to, without a speck of shame.

She can think of herself as gorgeous.
Because that's what Sammy had said.

He'd texted her at lunchtime, explaining how he wouldn't be able to come around tonight, because he'd been late this morning, and didn't want to anger Jim by being late tomorrow too. He'd also said that he was sorry, but that *I miss you gorgeous :) x* and so Donna didn't mind.

That much.

She's got him in her head, and he's got her in his, and she's already half-way out of it and so she doesn't mind that much.

The beanbag crumples underneath her, and her cotton pyjamas wrinkle against it. She runs her free hand across them both, enjoying the difference in texture, in weight.

She hasn't felt like getting dressed. Not properly.

There is still just about enough food in the fridge and in the cupboards that she won't have to bother heading out to the shop. There aren't any more stains on her new dress in need of dry-cleaning.

She has three good bottles of wine left in the store-cupboard.

If she can't see Sammy, then there's no need to go out.

Her mother had called about going round for dinner again tomorrow, but again she'd let it go through to answerphone. She'd erased the invitation, then turned the answerphone to mute. And drawn the curtains again, while she was standing so close. To save her having to do it later.

As she stepped back she'd caught her heel on something that felt like a root jutting out of the floor, and nearly ended up going arse over tit. Or tit over arse. It was just one of the legs of her swivel chair, it turned out, but it could have been nasty.

She's much safer down here.

There's a small jar of green olives on the bottom shelf of the nearest bookcase. A fork sticking out of the top like a flagpole, like the one on the church with the dragon slayer's cross.
Or a chimney. The jar itself a little cottage in another clearing up ahead.
A chicken-leg house, like Baba Yaga's.
Or a bog-standard hovel, disingenuously drab, like the kind owned by Merlin the wizard himself.

Books fan out in an arc around the front of the beanbag, as though she has already visited one of those figures and asked their advice. Pulled those disparate tomes at random from her shelves, not quite clear in the gloaming, and dealt them like a tarot hand.
A little trick to tell her fortune.

It's akin to waiting at the traffic lights, for Donna.

Red devil or green angel?

She will simply have to smile and take it as it comes.

She sets her wine glass down beside the jar of olives, and leans forward and flips over the book to the left. Bringing it closer to her face, she takes note of the cover – red, stretched canvas weave – and the title embossed there in faded gold print.

She has read this book four times.

She knows its narrative almost by heart.

She is glad that she picked it, albeit accidentally.

It takes place in a land not dissimilar to Spain, at the arse-end of the fourteenth century. It is more of a chivalric romance than a fairy tale in the strictest Brothers Grimm or Perrault manner.

But it's fantastical and mystical enough for it to make the grade, for Donna.

She sips her wine and steps inside.

32

S he discovers first the details of the dust. The swell and the squall of it, the whirling dervish ravaging across the river's empty bed. The whipping against her stallion's chestnut-coloured flank, and the whinny he gives in response. The stinging of the grit that slips between the eye-slits in her visor. The acrid taste of that which somehow ends up in her mouth.

The coughing that follows.

The tiredness that follows, that hounds her and her steed as this dust hounds the land. It saps her health, it takes her water. It steams her within her armour, and draws cracks upon her skin.

She feels not that she's been sleeping, but that she has been awake a hundred years. A thousand.

The lance in her left hand is tilted only at the earth.

After a time, the dust subsides, dissipating until it's little more than a shadow in their past. The horse's and hers. The land, apparently unaware that the menace has ceased its tormenting, remains steadfastly desolate, without hint of relief. Not so much as a puddle lies anywhere in sight.

Only a palimpsest of tracks and trails, which seem so grossly over-cluttered as to be written in a foreign tongue. Any possible escape route has been lost in translation.

As a knight accustomed to such barrenness as this, she had long ago been schooled to follow the insects and the birds to find a source of water.

Yet the insects are doing nothing but biting her horse's rump, and seeking out chinks in her chainmail and visor. And the birds don't do much except wheel high above them, calling out noises that sound too much like her name.

Raising her visor, she welcomes even this slight breeze upon her skin.

The insects, of course, seize on the opening, speeding towards it.

Her lashes bat back at them.

Her breath hurricanes them away, though not for so long.

She is weak, getting weaker, and wants only the sun upon her face a final time before she breaks.

The flies can have her then.

The birds and the worms and the other beasts also.

But not before.

She did not become a celebrated, valiant knight errant by giving up on life so easily.

They sing her name in taverns from the bluest Aegean to the Straits of Gibraltar; from the Gothic steppes to London's mud. Troubadours have, on making her acquaintance, been humbled into silence, before begging her to make her mark upon their scrolls, or on their harps.

In the fame stakes, in this region, at this time, even the great Prester John has got nothing on her.

Yet this mention of taverns gives Donna, on her beanbag, pause.

She swigs straight from the bottle, unable now or simply too lazy to bother with the hassle of refilling her glass.

Shame this doesn't slake her thirst within the desert.

If anything, it makes it worse.

This knightly version of her is taunted by the merest thought of such a draught. Tormented by pastoral fantasies of Frenchmen, shirtless and sweating, squashing grapes between their toes.

But, lo, what miracles might come to Donna Creosote the knight, out here in Spanish sand. The insects suddenly depart her flesh. The birds screech *war-ter, war-ter* now, swinging a scimitar's arc away to the east.

Her steed's ears prick up. His whinnying grows louder, much more insistent.

Donna pats his flank. She knows it too.

It's ok. It's ok.

Hauling on the reins, she alters their heading. Adding to their unexpected fortune, the scarified sandstone embankment dips up ahead, affords them a less hazardous escape from the trench than they had any right or reason to expect.

In the sky – so harsh in its blue that it troubles the eyes – the dark dots of the birds still loiter and swirl. They are perhaps a mile away, but they have stopped again to circle. Beneath their orbit, the surface shimmers.

Another blue, much calmer than the sky's, is settled out there on the plain.

It is, most assuredly, an ocean.

Donna Creosote, the great and worthy knight, has seen her share of oceans. Recognises the verity of this vision. So closely does it resemble the other oceans she has seen, in fact, that it could be a memory.

But, brave as ever, she trusts that it is not.

She spurs the bony flanks of her stallion, harder and harder, but he merely whinnies once more and staggers to a stop. He's well beyond the point of tired. His haunches are sagging and his forelegs have failed. He can't go on, not this dehydrated.

She dismounts, strokes her right gauntlet from dusty neck to dusty rump.

She raises his left ear and whispers: *Don't worry. I will be back with water.*

She fully intends to.
She is a woman of her word.

Half a mile into this trek, half a mile out from where those bastard birds all circle, and she begins to know the weight, the beyond-the-point-of-tiredness feeling that settled on her horse.

Iron is not fit clothing for such brimstone-heated climes as this.

Or it is the only clothing suitable: the shackles of the damned.

Slowly she lays down her lance, removes her armour. Helmet first, then plate by plate. Soon, she sports nothing but a coarse sacking shirt and coarse sacking pants.

Glancing at the harsh blue of the sky again, the harsher, blanker whiteness of the sun, she guesses even this will be too much.

Glancing at the calm of the ocean, she doesn't think she'll need it.

In anticipation of the cooling tide, she sets off at a pace she can't possibly maintain.

And yet, a quarter mile out, there she is, still going, still running with her arms out wide to greet the waves, as though they were a husband or a father coming home.

Such sweet potential in the burning air!

She forgets that she has neither of those things, forgets her universe is, at present, little beyond her own weak self and a thirsty, dying horse.

She throws her arms around that forgetting.

She hugs it in tight to her breast.

She is kind to it, gifts it the sound of her heart.

Which races.

Which war-drums.

Which battering-ram-beats at the inner wall of her chest.

The birds are so close now that she can hear their calls clearly.

War-ter.

War-ter.

She takes comfort and confidence from the fact that they have not yet reverted to calling her name.

She refuses to stop.

Refuses even to slow down.

Breath barely enters her lungs before the jolt of her feet on the sandstone expels it.

It doesn't matter to this fearless knight.

Donna Creosote does not give up. Does not surrender.

To any enemy. Man or beast or element.

Except, it seems, despair.

The glimmering expanse of ocean, blue and calm as eyes of all-forgiving gods, it keeps on falling further back, the nearer she gets to the place where it was.

At first, she doesn't want to admit that she knows what's happening.

But then she collapses, and has no other choice.

The earth is not cooling and blue as she lies there: it is wretched and red.

In the mirage she glimpses the traffic-light devil.

She screams vengeance upon him before she blacks out.

In this pause, this lull in proceedings, Donna uses the fork as a miniature lance, skewering an olive from deep in the jar.

She bites it in half.

The last thing she expects is to open her eyes and find herself living. The next to last thing she expects to find is someone else alongside her, living as well.

It is a man, and he is offering her water, from a leather bag.

She nods graciously to accept it, then snatches it out of his hand.

He introduces himself while she quenches her thirst.

His name is Samuel.

Her drinking done, she gives him a smile.

Until she remembers she's not wearing clothes.

Looking down the length of her sunburnt body, her feet look large again, look weird. She covers her breasts and her pubis, instinctively.

Samuel's eyes widen. He is embarrassed, on her behalf as much as his own. He turns away to help her hide her shame.

They sit there on the sandstone, not talking.

She hears the birds again overhead.

They have come to break the silence, she thinks.
And they will do so with a word that isn't *war-ter*.

She places her hand on the rough woollen shirt that covers his shoulder.
Will you help me get back to my horse? Will you give my steed a drink?

Will you give my steed a drink? repeats Donna, in the quiet of her flat.

Woah, boy.

Samuel grins and helps her to stand.

33

They sip from the same flagon of mead using separate straws. Around them, the tavern is a-bustle with gossip and murmurs of secrets and dangers and awestruck retellings of their magnificent deeds. The other patrons all watch them out the corners of their eyes, as if expecting another such deed to be done.

Here too, the air burns with potential.

Catches fire even easier, perhaps, due to the fumes of the beer and the regulars' sweat.

She should slow down with the wine, she thinks, holding the bottle up to the light. There's only a quarter of it left, maybe less, and the other two bottles will have to last her all night.

Still, she takes one more swig.

They are both waiting for something to happen, too.

They – the pair of them – are waiting for a man to meet them here at midnight and deliver them a map. On this map, so the old man, a pedlar, promised, is marked the location of a glorious treasure. *The kind of treasure you can only dream of*, he'd said.

They have adventure in their blood, this knight and her squire, and are inclined to believe wild lines of that sort.

The alternative, after all, is that there are no more quests to be had.

Just before the witching hour, the tavern door swings open.

A gust of wind and a hooded figure enter together: close as lovers, thick as thieves.

The gossip and the murmurs cease. The tale-telling is muted.

All eyes are on this shade, as he walks – no, walks is not right: he *slinks* – towards the bar. Even in this silence, nobody can pick up exactly what he says to the innkeeper, but the innkeeper, a bear of a man, turns swiftly and fetches a bottle of his finest liquor from the shelf. Produces a glass from underneath the counter, spits in it, polishes it with his rag.

The hooded figure leaves the glass and takes the bottle.

No gold changes hands.

The liquid sways and eddies in that bottle, as the hooded figure slinks again towards a table in the corner. The darkest recess of the hall. He sits, with steadiness and poise, and, once seated, he turns to face the room.

His eyes, though hidden, meet unblinking with a hundred others.

Ninety-six of those eyes turn away.

As soon as Donna and Samuel have joined him, he extends his hand in courtesy to both. Its grip is strong for that of a man they both know to be aged.

Before they begin, he lowers his hood. Another act of politeness or simply part of the ritual of deals such as this, they cannot be sure. Although, with the shadow as deep as it is, they still cannot clearly discern more than a few of his wrinkles. Like incomplete runes on a weatherworn rock.

It doesn't matter.

All that's important is that he's brought them the map.

He lays it out on the table, pinning it flat on one side with his liquor, and at the other with their mead.

He taps the tanned hide with a long, bony finger.

This is where we are, he says.

He drags his finger over a line that, in this dimness, they can barely make out.

This is where you'll have to go, he says. His voice is careworn, weatherbeaten as his face. Reminds them of grandparents they'd both once-upon-a-time known.

His finger comes to a halt, jabs the map twice for emphasis.

This is where you want to be.

Not quite true.

In this second book, she knows, the treasure's buried somewhere different than she wants to go today.

In another country, in other halls.

Sammy sent her a message a few minutes ago, asking how she was doing, saying sorry again that he can't visit tonight.

If he can't come round here, she thinks, then she will meet him in the castle. She will take him there and show him everything she knows.

They politely decline the map the pedlar is offering, but gladly stick around to help him finish the booze.

34

They leave the tavern at sun-up and make good time on the road.

Her steed is back to his old self again, powerful and lithe as he ranges cross-country. Hoofbeats like cannon-fire on the cobbles and flagstones. Iron of the horseshoes striking up sparks.

Samuel's steed is less mighty, less of a stallion and more of a mule.

But that's fine. She has assured him that he doesn't need to compensate for anything.

The mountains stand bold and blue in the distance, beyond the peaks of redwood pines. And, atop the highest mountain, the castle sits. Proud and rich and holding the only treasure that Donna Creosote desires.

The branches of the trees soon close out the view, though, soon shut out the sky. Sunlight only reaches the ground-level flora in shards that spear in through the canopy, thinner and thinner the further they go. Filamentary. Silken. Donna's horse whickers in delight whenever they pass through one of those.

Donna herself must admit that there is something mystical about them. They fork through her visor and bring a smile to her face.

She doesn't turn to check, but thinks that Samuel will be smiling, too.

They pause in the occasional clearings and look around, the way the poets recommend. They study these spaces, these arboreal cloisters, and a certain peace descends upon them. An ease with being. They feel cushioned from the nearby towns, from the fustiness and unsavoury intentions of that tavern and its clientele.

Such birds as there are in the higher branches don't call out names, or any words, but simply trade in melodies.

At some point, however, those melodies stop. They can't say when, for certain, because they can't see the sun. They stop reaching clearings. The shards of light stop breaking through.

Donna's steed becomes hesitant, reticent, slowing down and whinnying not with pleasure but with fear. Samuel's mount starts to tremble and squirm.

The great knight's eyes become accustomed to the gloom; she starts to notice that the tree trunks here are rotten, even though the uppermost branches still appear to be growing, still appear to be healthy, covered with leaves.

Other eyes flicker and lurk in the darkness: the eyes of small animals too frightened to move.

Then a sudden rustle in the undergrowth, and all of them scatter.

She hauls on the reins, attempting to steer her horse back where they've come from, but a horde of bandits has already burst forth from the undergrowth, shouting *Your money or your life!* as they close round in a ring.

Donna and Samuel pull their steeds to a halt, there being no room to gather the speed to escape.

Their bandit captors point and laugh, and dance around the hapless heroes, a carnival of silhouettes with leering grins and crooked knives. Coming closer and closer.

Closer
and
closer.

So close that Donna can discern at last their dirty bandit faces, even as they dodge about and try to hide them in the gloom.

With each recognition, she feels herself twist.

Samuel is clueless, overwhelmed, looking to her for ideas on how they might yet survive.

He shimmies his mule nearer, side by side with her stallion.

She can reach across and touch his shoulder, pat his back to calm him down.

No fear, she says, as she readies for battle.

Because this time the knight errant has remembered her sword.

35

The pathway up the mountain is blocked and guarded by far too many men.

Donna Creosote may be a bold and celebrated hero, but she isn't bloody daft.

They will have to climb the cliff instead.

Be back soon, she whispers confidentially, confidently, into the upraised ear of her horse.

Samuel just pats his mule on the rump and says: *See ya.*

Halfway up the rock-face she begins to feel funny.
Not haha funny, but strange.
Her helmet grows increasingly tight on her head.

When she stops still against the mountain, Samuel, ever-attentive, looks over.

What's wrong? he asks.

She doesn't know.

She's never felt like this before.

They press on, Samuel watching her closely all the while. Donna is touched, if a little unnerved, by the depth of his concern.

The way he looks at her, it makes her feel as if there's something he can see that he isn't letting on.

She wants to ask if that's the case, and why he doesn't just come out and tell her, but feels that a vertical plane two hundred feet above sea-level might not be the best place for them to have their first fight.

Shortly before the top, she pauses again.
She cannot carry on like this.
Her helmet is squeezing her skull like a vice.
Holding on tight to the rock with one hand, she unfastens her headgear, takes it off, lets it drop.

Set free, a stream of bright copper unspools from her head.
Spills back down the side of the mountain like lava.

Her hair has grown. Is still growing, in fact.

Samuel looks on, agog.
He had seen the feathers of it peeking from under the metal, but harboured no hopes of such glory as this.
He is entranced.
Her mane, to him, is mesmerising.

So much so that he misses a handhold,
                                        and falls.

But he catches the end of her ponytail, and she has to carry him the rest of the way.

They will have their first fight, she thinks, as soon as they both reach the top.

When they get there, however, the castle gates are unguarded.
Wide open.

As they pass beneath the portcullis, Donna Creosote's armour begins to weigh heavy again. But this is a different heaviness from that which struck her in the desert. It comes not out of weakness, but rather from a sudden knowing that she doesn't need it anymore.

Not here.

Not with all the soldiers gone to watch the mountain path.

She hands her sword to Samuel for safekeeping, and casts off the breastplate, the gauntlets, the greaves.

He takes a step backwards to better appraise her. To see how she looks in her new satin gown.

Gorgeous, he says. She believes him and blushes.

But, she thinks, with an inner grin, he'd have preferred it if more had come off.

She grabs hold of him, laughing, and they kiss beneath the chandelier. They run barefoot towards the marble stairs, their footsteps making echoes that harmonise around them.

After a whistle-stop, whirligig tour of the premises, they sprint down a corridor to the large double-doors. Dark-varnished oak with gold-plated handles.

After you, she says.

He twists one of the handles and then steps aside, bowing.

No, my lady, after you.

The silver candelabras provide the mood lighting, as before.

She fancies she hears harpists strumming jaunty softcore funk.

But no, it's the phone.

The landline.

Ringing and ringing and ringing some more.

She knows without getting up and looking at the small display screen exactly who's calling.

Her mother, pestering her about going round tomorrow for Sunday lunch.

The amount of wine she's drunk, she isn't going to be awake by lunchtime, and, besides, she really doesn't want to go. She doesn't want to meet Bob, or spend time with her mother. All she wants to do is wait it out until Sammy can come back.

The phone rings off.

She tries to return to the castle, but all she finds when she does is that they didn't get the treasure and now they're being chased.

36

They are trapped in a dungeon.
For a while, they puzzle out the dank and mossy paths by torchlight. The flame casts whorish red against the stonework, highlighting the white of bones that sit like malformed stars within the dark.

Donna counts them. Names them. Ribs and skulls and spines and ulnas. They tumble loose from the walls as the prisoners pass, they clatter and scrape and congeal in the shadows. They form traffic-light devils and stand in the way.

Stop. they whisper, each in turn.

It is not safe to pass here.

Donna and her squire should, perhaps, consider taking these devils' advice.

But then the torch goes out.

And something else inside the darkness bellows.

A distant noise, maybe, but not distant enough.

It bellows again.
A tortured groaning, rising from a throat that they call tell is scarcely human.

Donna knows exactly what it is, of course.

She knew which book she'd get this time, before she even turned it over.

She'd stacked the deck.

It's the illustrated compendium of myths that Sammy returned to her last night.

The howling, lowing ululation the beast gives out is drawing closer, as they huddle tight in Daedalus' labyrinth and pledge a tragic lover's vow.

If the Minotaur finds us, don't let it take me alive.

Don't let it take me alone.

If this were a cellar instead of a maze, then maybe they'd make that promise with wine.

They try running back the way they came, but soon reach a dead end. Donna's hands trace the walls, but can find no break or secret panel. No space through which the two of them might safely squeeze to freedom. They turn and turn, disoriented by the darkness, the way that everything, in every direction, all appears the same, in that it doesn't appear at all. By the fact that they can know each other here by touch and smell and sound alone.

In a different locale, that thought might be tantalising, but in this labyrinth, the loss of sight – the vanishing of each other's face – brings out a terror that, for Donna, presages what it must be like to die.

Condemned to lumber, lovelorn, through the chill kingdom of Hades, confronting the same old sweet nothing again and again.

The bellowing grows closer.

Echoes spread across the dungeon walls like ripples on the Styx.

And, for once, Donna Creosote, the great knight, adventurer, *raconteur*, lover, can't conceive of a way out.

Saved by the bell.

Well, by the phone.

She guesses it's her mother again, asking the same question.

Checking, just to make sure.

She guesses as well that her mother will keep checking, unless she gets up and does something about it. She disentangles herself from the beanbag, nearly knocking over the two-thirds empty wine bottle, her second, in the process.

She sways towards her desk, where the phone is currently located, and steadies herself by placing her hands on the back of the chair as she waits for the call to ring off. When it does, she grabs the receiver, navigates into the menu, and sets the ringer volume to mute.

It's ok, she thinks. Sammy only has my mobile number.

By the time she slumps down again, she's come up with an answer.

As they spin, as they twist, as they dance a rattled tango, something winds about their bodies, constricting and taut.
Samuel's heartbeat hammers against her.
Her nipples get hard and her own pulse rate spikes.

But she stops short of panic when she feels a tug on her scalp, because she realises they're only caught up in her hair.

She must have snagged her ponytail on a gatepost by the entrance.

She tells Samuel, and they unravel themselves, before gathering the ponytail in their hands and working back along its length. Better than yarn, Donna thinks, because a ball of yarn could be dropped and lost within this murk forever.

The lowing, the bass howling, is dying away.

There is a sliver of light up ahead. Compared to the grave-black of the labyrinth, its clarity and brightness appear absolute.

As they draw nearer it expands, and, in the hush, they feel like witnesses to some strange and sacred re-enactment of the universe's start.

Sure enough, when they pass into it, through it, they discover for themselves a brand new world.

37

D runk as she is, Donna isn't unaware of how long, roughly, she's been dreaming today.

The fourth book she turns over is another illustrated edition, but this time one that had been loved more in her own childhood than in Sammy's.

Sometimes she had read beneath a tent that she made with her duvet, by pulling it across from her bed to her drawers. She fixed it at one end by jamming it in the top drawer and at the other by pinning it beneath the mattress, she shuffled underneath with her bedside lamp and began to flip the pages.

Flipping the first page today reveals a picture of a dragon.

The brave and noble knight-princess, Donna Creosote, stands out in the centre of a town square, beside a fountain. Still wearing her gown, her hair still copper-coloured and winding out behind her like a molten stream across the flagstones.
Her squire stands beside her, fearless and tall.

The labyrinth has changed him for the better, Donna decides. Surviving the Minotaur has made him tougher in the head.

A much needed quality, she thinks, given the ferocious mass of the dragon that currently claws at the courtyard before them.

Given how, when it stretches its wings to their full span, they are double the size of the town hall that squats, shambolic, behind.

Given how its eyes are the size of horses' heads, and its nostrils gape like oubliettes.

Given how each talon is the size of a two-handed sword.

Which, once again, neither Donna Creosote nor Samuel currently possess.

More's the pity.

The dragon fills its cavernous lungs and lets loose with a hideous roar.

Drunk as she is, Donna remains conscious of how consistently peril has featured in her fantasies today. Conscious too that this is far from unusual. She has considered at length, several times, the fact that so many fairy tales need such peril in order to function.

The fact that, in so many of those fairy tales and fantasies and myths, such peril serves a dual purpose. It is there to give entertainment and excitement to the audience, and to help move the story along. But it is also there to give excitement to the characters themselves: in particular, the romantic leads.

All of this danger is foreplay for the honeymoon at the end.

So far, however, it has been the courageous and celebrated Donna Creosote who has been doing most of the work. Who has been putting in most of the effort, as far as this foreplay's concerned.

She is looking now to her squire to step up and do what needs to be done.

To get his hands dirty.

Only, when she turns to face him, he isn't there.
He isn't in front of her either.

And she doesn't think he's been eaten.
Yet.

He has run away on her, then. At the last, and worst, moment.
After all that they've been through, he's just upped sticks
and fled.
Revealed himself, like the others, to be more boy than man.

Donna drops an olive in her mouth, washes it down with the
start of the third bottle, some of which spills across her chin,
drips down her neck and stains the collar of her pyjamas.

She doesn't notice, and probably won't until morning.

This is not uncommon to Donna Creosote. This being alone.
She's not unaccustomed to playing the lone wolf, to being
the last woman standing.
In fact, she's far more accustomed to this than to the
alternative state: being fully able to rely and depend upon
another person; being able to trust that other person with her
safety, her life.

Why else would she have been wandering with only her
horse over oven-baked earth in the first place?

Lonely are the brave, indeed.
But not, Donna thinks now, because there are so few of them
around.
They are not lonely because they're brave.
They are brave because they're lonely.
Because people with proper friends, proper lovers, have
them there to warn them off from doing stupid shit like this.

Small and fragile-seeming in her satin gown, Donna Creosote barely reaches as high as the middle of the dragon's shin. She glances around the square for anything or anyone that she can use to help her. For anything at all that she can take to hand to give herself a fighting chance.

A pocket-knife some schoolkid's dropped.

A weighty purse.

A pebble, even.

But there is nothing of the sort.

The dragon inhales again, drawing itself up to full height, spreading its wings. From the red glow in its nostrils, she can tell that it's about to breathe fire.

She dives in to the left.

Just behind where she'd been standing, the fountain water fizzles in a geyser of steam.

The dragon, seeing her flat on the ground, claws its way towards her.

Two steps and it's within range.

The shadow of its foot is a total eclipse.

Donna is back to the darkness of the forest, the darkness of the maze. The promised darkness of Hades and the deep River Styx.

But then, the shadow recedes.

There is panic, there are the sounds of wings the size of buildings battering the air.

Roaring that comes forth not as a threat, but as a worry.

The noise of walls and roofs collapsing, and of something even bigger crashing down into the dust.

The aftershocks continue for a minute, and, all the while, Donna Creosote, famed and matchless warrior that she is, lies paralysed with fear upon the stone.

Until, that is, she feels the slightest of pulls at the back of her head.

Once again, Samuel's soft hand reaches to help her.

His grin seems to light up the whole of his face and, contagious, it lights hers up too.

He pulls her to her feet and gestures at the desolation.

The town square is a shit-heap.

Like so many she's known.

Is this the way they always get like that? she wonders.

Unlike others, however, this town square has a sleeping dragon in the heart of it, tail spliced neatly through the middle of what was, not long ago, the mayor's place of work.

And, around the neck of the dragon, having been used to choke it into a slumber, is a lasso that Samuel had fashioned out of Donna's fiery hair.

When the dragon awakes, somewhat dazedly, it's startled to find its conquerors saddled on its neck, that ponytail now rigged up as reins and harness, clamping around its crocodilian jaws.

Too concussed to harbour thoughts of vengeance, and not wishing to be beaten for the second time in a day, it agrees to transport them swiftly to a romantic retreat of their choice.

They hold on tight as the dragon takes a running start skywards; only when it levels out are they able to relax.

They breathe deeply.

They smile.

They pull closer and kiss.

Then pull closer still.

In the darkness of the living room, Donna rubs herself to sleep.

38

Once her head had calmed, and her stomach settled, Donna Crick-Oakley checked the time.

Half-past two meant that she'd overslept any chance of joining her mother for Sunday lunch. Meant also that her mother would likely have left another few messages for her to ignore.

Donna didn't feel guilty. She'd told her mother before that she wasn't interested in meeting these new men. If her mother didn't listen, and became disappointed when Donna declined to attend, then it was her mother's fault, and her mother's problem.

She made herself a cup of coffee using two teaspoons of instant rather than her usual one, she sat down at the table, where she appeared to have left her mobile the night before, and checked her texts.

She had three from Sammy, but none from anybody else. She'd given her mother her mobile number for emergencies, but her mother didn't have a mobile herself – she preferred to sit at home in a comfy chair when she talked to her friends – and always claimed that she couldn't find the number, or that Donna had written it down for her wrong.

Maybe she had.

Two of Sammy's texts were from last night, and one from an hour or so ago, when he must have been on his lunch break. The first from last night asked what she was up to, and apologised again for not being able to come round. The second asked if she was alright, and said that, if she'd fallen asleep already, that was ok, because *I'm pretty knackered as well ;) x*

The one from lunchtime seemed far more concerned, and was, in itself, far more concerning.

Hey Donna are you ok? Is everything alright? Hope I haven't said owt wrong...let me know when you get this, ok? xx

She felt daft for not checking her phone more last night.

She knew how quickly a thing like not receiving fast replies near the beginning of a relationship could play on a person's mind, and she'd neither meant nor wanted to make him worry or make him start apologising all over again.

But then, it wasn't good to know that his response to that kind of situation was to overcompensate. To assume, firstly, that he'd done something wrong; and, by implication, that anything affecting her mood or actions had to be his fault, or at least his doing.

And, secondly, that the best way to fix that was to add an extra *x* to the end of the message.

That second kiss, that made everything more serious still.

It made the non-problem of her being too inebriated to reply the night before into a problem that needed solving. It made the quick-fix solution to that problem a reply with the same amount of kisses.

Or more, if she felt guilty enough, which she didn't.

And, in doing so, it made their relationship into something more adult, more rational, more caring, more dependant.

If she only sent one kiss with her reply, even if she replied to the effect that nothing was wrong, she'd just been tired, then not only would he think he'd made another mistake, but he would remain unconvinced that things between them were ok.

But, if she sent two, she'd be letting him know that she was fine with things moving that little bit faster. And, because he'd been the one who'd jumped to that level first, she'd be letting him dictate the pace of play.

She did find herself missing him, though.
She found herself wanting the hours between now and this evening to just rush right on by.

She waited until she'd finished her coffee before responding.

Hey Sammy, I was tired, yeah lol ;) Have only just got up... Looking forward to seeing you later! Please bring wine :) xx

39

It was the smell of smoke that had brought her out to the balcony. The threat and the possibility of the building being alight.

If this is it, she thought, then maybe they'll send the ladders up.

If Rapunzel had had hair as short as mine, she thought, then her prince would have had to do the same.

Wearing her dressing gown over her pyjamas, she was swaying just slightly with her hands on the rails.

The smoke was from a barbecue three floors below. Despite the thickness of its scent, Donna fancied she could smell the beer and the tomato ketchup too. Although, to be honest, she preferred brown sauce.

Barbecues weren't technically allowed, as far as Donna understood the contract, but days as fine as this were such rare beasts around here that not having one would have been an absolute waste. A dereliction of duty.

She contemplated sending another text to Sammy, asking him to pick up a disposable barbecue when he went for the wine, but decided against it.

By the time he arrived, the sun would be down and the air would be cold.

Maybe wet as well.

Away to the east, it looked like clouds were sweeping in.

Music reached her, belatedly, with the burger-fat scent.

'Mr Brightside,' she could tell. She'd heard that often, back in the day. She was swaying to the music, not the lyrics. They didn't apply to her. She wasn't the jealous type.

She watched the arrow-straight passing of cars down below. The hum of their engines came up through the music. A droning backbeat; a dubstep whump.

People moved to and fro on the pavement, not particularly quickly. One of them, heading to the right, in the direction of the football stadium, was pushing a pram. Donna thought it was the woman she'd met in the lift.

She wondered if the baby's father lived with them.

Or if, when she headed out that way, she was going to visit him, spend some time together. Catch up and watch their child grow.

Donna hoped it was one or the other.

But she didn't want to think about children. Not yet.

Not about their crying, or their living, or their being cared for and raised by consenting adults.

She didn't want to start getting anything like broody.

Even though the sun was out, the same air currents that brought the smoke up past her window carried a slight chill. Normally, it wouldn't have been cold enough to bother her, but, fragile as she felt today, she was thankful for the extra layer, the soft woollen collar brought up close to her throat.

She didn't know what she'd wear later, for Sammy.

She had plenty of outfits that he hadn't seen yet, but most were far closer to the level of her jeggings and boob-tube combination than they were to her dark green dress. She couldn't wear that dress again for him just yet, she thought, but neither could she wear the boob-tube, and so she'd have to try and pick out something in between.

A broad gulf.

She worried about this because she wanted to look nice for him, rather than because she thought he'd judge her if she didn't try.

He had traced his finger along her collarbone before he left her on Saturday. Kissed it.
Kissed her mouth after. Morning breath and all.

The same breeze that brought the scents of smoke and beer and ketchup to Donna ruffled her hair against her cheek. She hadn't got round to showering yet, and so it was still matted and thick with sweat. She pulled her fingers through it, winced as she tugged out a few of the knots.
If her hair really was that much longer, she thought, how much time would it take to clean? How would she get it all in the shower?
It'd probably be easier to let it form into dreadlocks.

If she did that, she thought, it'd make a much better rope.

Donna knew there were a few hours to go until seven, but still she looked down again towards the street.
She wondered whether she should come back out before Sammy arrived, let him know that she'd been waiting for him. See if he looked up towards her flat before buzzing the door. See if he noticed she was there.
Wave at him.
Get him to wave back.

So much great romance began with balconies, or at least that was what so much of great literature had told her.

Had been telling her, over and over, ever since she was ten.

That was the age at which little Donna Creosote had begun reading the great tragedies, that one in particular, in fair Verona, where we lay our scene. Her father, the English teacher, so desperate for her to *get a headstart on all the thickies in secondary school*. So keen for her to learn how to do different voices for each character; so eager for her to learn how to act, how to lie.

When she'd struggled, at first, with the language and with the length of the plays, her father had called her a thickie and said she was just like the rest. Worse, even. When she'd taken such admonishment poorly, he'd called her a cry-baby and gone off to watch TV.

Bloody Shakespeare.

40

Donna Creosote opened the door wearing nothing but her dressing gown.

Sammy was standing there with both hands behind his back.

She stopped herself from throwing her arms around him. Looked at him funny.

Whatcha hiding? she said.

He withdrew his left hand first, plastic bag hanging from it, and the silhouette of a wine bottle dancing within.

In his right hand he held a white cardboard box, the kind that often contained cakes.

Surprise, he said.

Awww, you shouldn't have.

She took them both from him, and told him to follow her in and shut the door.
As she placed them down upon the table, she felt his hands reach out to settle on the angles of her hips.

I've missed you, he whispered.

Unfastened her dressing gown, let it fall to the floor.

41

It was only when they returned to the kitchen that Donna took a closer look at the box.

Inside was a pie, not a cake.

What's in it?

What?

What's the filling?

Special.

Special?

Just wait and see.

Is it fish?

It's a type of fish, yeah, but just wait and see.

I thought we went over this. I said I didn't like them.

I know, I know. I was listening to you, honest.

Were you?

Yeah, but, seriously, just try it. I had Jim make it for you specially, using a recipe I'd come up with myself. It's not like I've just brought it round because I got it free, either. It's come out of my wages.

Aww, really?

Yeah. Just thought it might be nice for you to try one. Two of the old ladies who bought them yesterday came back to the stall today and said how nice they were and asked if they could get another next week.

Oh, that's good.

Yeah. And they were just regular ones, not this special mix that me and Jim put together for you.

Ok. Sorry — I didn't mean to sound ungrateful or anything. It's just that I'd said I didn't like them —

It's alright. It's ok. I reckon you'll like this one, though. And if you don't, there's always the wine.

Hang on, I said sorry but I didn't say I was going to eat it.

C'mon. You won't know unless you try, will you?

She'd been fooled with lines like that before.

Ok.

Ok? That mean we're good to go? Can I put it in the oven?

Well — only if you agree to do something in return.

Name it.

I noticed the other night that you didn't touch any of the olives I'd put out.

And?

I'd like you to try them. You know, in exchange for me trying this pie.

I have tried them. They're manky.

When? When did you try them? How long ago?

When I was like eight, or something. What does that matter?

Your tastebuds adapt and alter as you get older.

And?

It's been years since you last tried them – you might feel differently if you have them now.

I won't. My tastebuds might have adapted and whatnot, but olives will always be manky.

Well, you won't know for sure unless you try, will you?

...

See, you'll have to do it now. So there.

    She stuck her tongue out.
    Something about the moment felt like being nine again, in the playground.

Maybe she could ask him to do that, instead. To play Little Red Riding Hood. He could be the woodcutter or the wolf, she didn't really mind.

Ok, I'll do it. But I'm only having one.

Too late.

One olive for one pie? That doesn't seem fair now, does it?

Yeah, well, that's what I'm offering. Take it or leave it.

Ooh, are you putting your foot down, all manly-like?

Damn right I am. Woman.

He stuck his tongue out right back.
Neither of them could keep from laughing.

As Sammy took the pie from the box, Donna unscrewed the top from the wine, started filling the glasses.

How should I cook this?

You don't know? I thought that was your job?

No, I mean, do you want me to put it in a tray, or not?

Isn't it in one already?

Yeah, but it's kind of spilling over the top. If you don't mind it spilling down to the bottom of your oven, then it should be fine.

No, don't want that. I always forget to clean it and it ends up burning next time I cook owt.

Well, I can clean it later, if you want?

You won't have time later. The trays are in the cupboard to the left of the cooker.

Ok, got one.

Ok.

Is this what you were wearing the other day?

What?

This tray. Was it part of what you were wearing?

Why? What does it matter?

No reason. Just curious.

Look, if you're going to start taking the piss, you can leave. And take your fuckin' pie with you.

What? What the fuck, Donna? I was only asking.

Don't *what the fuck* me. I thought we'd gone over all that. I thought you apologised and said it was cool and I thought we were leaving it at that.

I did. I am. For fuck's sake. I'm sorry. I'll tell you what, I won't talk. In fact, I think I will leave, and I'll take my fuckin' pie with me. How's that? And you can give me a call or whatever when you've calmed the fuck down.

Always fuckin' happens –

What always fuckin' happens?

This. Girls always just flip out and everything, when I try do something like this. Always.

Girls?

Yes, girls. You. You fuckin' – you fuckin' invite me round because, what, you're lonely or whatever, or you just want a shag, and then as soon as I start trying to do things for you, to act like we're in a fuckin' relationship, you snap and start screaming at me for no fuckin' reason –

I'm not screaming at you!

I'm not screaming at you.

Shouting then. Whatever, you're pissed off at me and I didn't do anything wrong. All I did was ask a question. That's all I ever fuckin' do, just ask stupid questions.

If that's all you ever do, then why don't you learn from your mistakes and stop asking them? And if you have to go home to do that, then go home.

You know what, Donna, fuck you. I was only asking because I'm interested in you, and if you don't want me to be, then it's nothing that a few beers and a night in front of the internet won't fix.

He was bundling the pie back into the box, knocking bits of crust off as he did so.

Once he'd forced the lid back on, he paused to down his glass of wine.

So, what, you're just going to walk out?

You just told me to walk out. It's pretty clear you like everything your own way, so, yeah, I think I'm going to go.

What if I told you to stay?

Are you telling me to stay?

I dunno. Are you going to apologise?

What the fuck? Apologise for what?

What do you mean *for what*? For fuckin' taking my pie! Bastard.

Oh, so now you want it?

Yeah, yeah, now I want it. I'm sure it's every bit as special as you say it is. I'm sure it's fuckin' magical.

Well, you'd fuckin' know all about that.

Yeah. Yeah, I would.

Good.

He held the pie box up, balanced on his palm.

Then

he let it fall.

It crumpled open when it landed, and most of the pie-filling spilled out on the floor.

It seemed to be salmon.

He turned for the exit.

Don't you dare leave, Sammy. Don't you fucking dare walk out that door!

He took hold of the handle.

C'mon, Sammy. Don't go.

Please.

Please don't go.

Please.

I'm sorry.

Please.

Please.

42

T he uncooked pie had dried overnight, and the salmon fairly stank. It took Donna nearly half of a kitchen roll and some anti-bac wipes to clear it up fully.

Once this was done, she took a quick swig of the leftover wine, and then headed into the bathroom again to wash her hands and brush her teeth.

In the mirror, the condensation revealed what was left of the heart.

Over their first coffee, neither said much.

They had made up three times last night, and once in the shower this morning.

He was upset about the pie, she knew, and she'd said sorry in as many ways as she could think of, but still he didn't seem ready to talk, not properly. When the second coffee was poured, they traded a few words, *two sugars* and *thank you*, but that was all.

He wasn't exactly glaring at her across the table, but neither was his face lit up the way she liked.

I put that armour on because I was bored, you know.

Sammy looked up from his drink, cocked his head.

I mean, I put it on because all I ever seem to do is daydream about things like that, and I just wanted to actually do it for once. To try and see how it feels, or might have felt, you know?

Sammy kept his mouth shut, kept looking at her funny.

I know that probably sounds crazy, trying to be a knight in 'uddersfield, or, like, a vigilante or whatever, and it sounded crazy to me too, when I was doing it. I mean, I knew how it would look to people, I think, but I wanted to do it anyway. It's like you said about it – you never see anyone doing anything like that in town.

I know what I said. And I meant it. I was a bit pissed when I was typing that message, but I meant what I said.

I know you did –

So why did you act like you didn't believe me yesterday? Why did you instantly jump to the conclusion I was taking the piss?

I don't know. It's just, old boyfriend stuff, you know. Like, when you have a few people mess you around, you tend to think that everyone else is going to do that as well.

What, so you're still not over your exes?

No.

No?

No. I mean, yes, I am over them. I didn't mean it like that.

Ok. So how did you mean it? Because I'll tell you now, I've got no interest in being a rebound or a stopgap or just marking time until the next guy comes along. I've been that too often, and it gets old, fast. So, if that's what's happening here, just tell me, please. Just be kind now and tell me that. Please.

Not like that, ok. Just calm down. All I meant was that I'd opened up to guys before about, you know, the things I like, and they've kind of shot it down. Like, my last boyfriend, Kirk, he didn't get why I had so many books, and he wanted me to take them out of my bedroom, said they 'creeped him out'. It's things like that. It's not you.

Ok. But, again, I told you I was cool with all that. I said I liked it, actually. So, I don't get why you flipped out at me like that, I'm sorry.

I know, I know. But it's just that —

What? That you thought I was lying to you? That you don't believe me when I say things to you? What?

No, it's not that at all.

Because I didn't need to take that photo offline, you know. I didn't put it up there to embarrass you, and if I had have done, you calling me a bastard would not have made me take it down. I don't lie about the things I like.

I know. I'm sorry, I know I was wrong. I was just tired, and I wasn't thinking clearly. I know you weren't taking the piss. I wouldn't have told you all the stuff I did if I thought you were the kind to take the piss.

Ok. I'm glad to hear you say that. I'm sorry too. I shouldn't have dropped the pie all over the place. I shouldn't have said the things I was saying. I don't get angry like that, usually. I was tired too. I don't like fights.

Me neither.

Well, just for the record, you are pretty good at them. You could go pro. Probably challenge for the title in a couple of years.

A couple of years? You trying to start another, or just wanting to train me up?

Train you. I'll throw in a montage sequence in a bit, make you run up some mountains.

Eh?

You know, like in Rocky IV?

Oh, right. No, never seen it.

Never? You are missing out, lass.

Really? Doesn't sound like my kind of thing.

Are you kidding? Rocky is everyone's kind of thing. It's fun for all the family.

I wouldn't know.

Aww, Donna, I'm sorry, I didn't mean it like that. I didn't think –

It's ok, don't worry about it. I don't want to talk about it.

Ok.

What I do want to talk about is how, when you dropped that pie, I think you did it just so you wouldn't have to try an olive. I think you tried to wind me up on purpose, just so you could get out of the deal.

Damn. You got me.

And there was a little bit of that light in his face that she wanted.

But you're not getting out of it that easily.

Aww, c'mon, it's breakfast time. No-one has olives for breakfast. That's grim.

Grim or not, buggerface, you're doing it.

Pie's gone, though, so you can't keep up your end of the bargain, which is totally unfair.

I'll do something else as my side of the deal.

What?

A surprise.

Ooh, what kind of surprise?

You'll find out when you're older. Now, are you ready?

Just so we're clear, if I eat one olive – he held up a finger to emphasise the number – *you're going to do something, you know, for me?*

We won't know until you eat the olive now, will we?

Ok. Bring it on.

Donna fetched the jar from the fridge, and when she shut the door she noticed a word on it: sorry.

She tried not to smile as she unscrewed the lid.

Taking an olive between finger and thumb, she shook off the excess brine and then leaned across the table.

Say ahh.

He opened his mouth, and she set the olive ceremoniously between his front teeth.

Then nodded.

He bit into it, slowly, the pimento exploding across the enamel.

His mouth wrinkling and twisting, his eyes closing tight.

See, you big wuss, it wasn't as bad as all that.

43

S ammy left the tower block mid-morning.
Monday and Tuesday were his days off, he said. They were kind of his own special weekend, he said. And he liked to spend most of them sleeping.

Donna stopped short of saying he could always *just sleep here.* It was maybe too soon for an offer like that.

Besides, sometimes people just needed space.

Sometimes they needed an ocean.

She hadn't been near her computer all weekend, to check her emails or social networks. Not that it was likely she'd have heard much from anyone, but it was, she reasoned, always worth having a look. Online booksellers, at least, might have sent through a few updates, and she did enjoy having a scout through the deals.

The chair sank when she sat in it, and the computer wheezed and whirred as it started.

The light that indicated her landline phone had voicemails was flashing, sitting there in its cradle next to the screen. She remembered turning the volume off the other night.

She wondered how many messages her mother would have left her about missing Sunday lunch.

Eight, the phone said, when she pressed the button.

She held the phone to her ear as they started to play.

Hi, love, it's your mum, just seeing how you are, and if you're coming over tomorrow? We'd really like to see you. Bob can't wait to meet you. (Saturday, 7:15 PM)

Hi, Donna, it's only me again. Can you let me know about lunch? I need to know which roast to get out. Bob fancies beef, or I've got a chicken in the freezer. (Saturday, 8:32 PM)

Hi, love, are you in? Is your phone working? Listen, I don't know whether you'd decided to come round later or not, but we're probably going to have to put it off til next week now. Bob's not feeling well. Call me back. (Sunday, 9:17 AM)

Hi, Donna, love, can you give me a call back on this number I'm calling from as soon as you get this. I've had to go into hospital with Bob. We had to get an ambulance. Everything's ok, love, but can you call me when you wake up? (Sunday, 11:26 AM)

Donna, pick up. Are you in? Donna. Donna, love, pick up. Pick up the phone, I need to talk to you. Can you come to the hospital? They've put Bob in the Cardiac Care Unit, I don't know what to do, they won't let me see him. His son's still on his way from Wales, won't be here for another hour or something because of traffic. Please call me back or just come here, I don't know what to do. (Sunday, 2:41 PM)

They're going to operate, Donna. He's just... The machine was beeping. The monitor. His face was blue, Donna. Bloody... blue. Where the fuck are you? Donna? (Sunday, 7:22 PM)

He's... he's dead, Donna. They just told – he's dead, he's had a heart attack and he's dead, Donna, and his son's here but he isn't speaking and I don't know what... Donna, I don't know what's happening. He was so healthy, he was so... Bob's dead, Donna. I can't go see him, Donna, I can't look at him like this on my own. I'm at the hospital and I need you Donna need – (Sunday, 10:17 PM)

Hello, is this the number for Donna Crick? This is Imelda, from Huddersfield Royal Infirmary. Your mother is refusing to leave the premises until you arrive, and we would very much like for you to come and collect her. We appreciate that she has recently suffered a loss, but she is upsetting some of our other visitors. Please get here as soon as you can, and ask at reception. (Today, 6:49 AM)

44

She skidded across the marble tiling, nearly went headfirst into the trees.

Wait.

Why the hell were there trees in here?

This was an entrance hall, not a bloody arboretum.
No. No, this was a bedroom.
Her bedroom.
She just hadn't turned the light on.

Why had she come here, though?

She bumped into the laundry basket, and remembered.
She reached into it, like reeling water from a well. She pulled out her jeggings and dropped them on the floor. A few pairs of knickers. A T-shirt. A silk pyjama top. Somewhere near the bottom, she found the work trousers, and after them the hoody.
Small scraps of duct-tape still clung to both, but she figured you could only see them, really, if you knew where to look. And anyway they were the warmest, neatest things she could find at such short notice. It was an outfit she felt ok going to Huddersfield Royal Infirmary in.

Donna Crick-Oakley had been born in that building.
She came into the maternity ward there as *a screaming pink goblin*, her father had said. Had said as well, though, that

she was the most beautiful goblin that anyone could have ever hoped to see.

Once.

A memory from before her school-life had started, when he hadn't felt the need to test her every night, and he was the one telling the stories himself.

Almost her earliest memory, in fact.

She stumbled back into the kitchen, wondering if she should have another cup of coffee. She was tired from last night, worn out from cleaning. She felt like she needed something just to help her stop shaking.

But she didn't have time.

She'd only been to the hospital on a couple of occasions.

She remembered going there when she'd broken her collarbone, obviously. The scratchy chair in the waiting room. The nurse calling her name.

She didn't remember anything at all about being born.

She'd heard about some people who claimed to recall exactly how things had been inside the womb. Who claimed to know precise sensations from their delivery, even down to the face of the doctor who helped them break out. Claimed to have recognised them years later, without so much as an introduction.

Donna was not such a person.

More and more, she felt as though she imagined her past as opposed to remembering it. She had the details, the bare facts, squirrelled away like favourite quotes; using them as a foundation, she could build up the scene afresh in her mind.

Different, a little, every time it played out.

Even so, there wasn't really anything that corresponded to this. That told her how to go about it.

Except, yes, yes there was. There was the time her grandma fell. The last time. And didn't know that she'd fallen.

She should call a taxi, she thought. She didn't want to mess about trying to reach the line of them that camped in the town centre. She had to have a number somewhere. A card, a leaflet.

There was nothing on the fridge, just the letters rearranged still to say sorry.

Perhaps on the shelves. She'd certainly made bookmarks out of weirder things.

A lot of the books on those shelves were essentially the same story. They involved the same, or at least similar, characters. Featured similar quests, similar conclusions. Had similar enemies and perils for the heroes and heroines to face. Similar triumphs and getaways for them to enjoy.

And yet she valued them all.

Their sameness, their shared fantasies, shared ideals, shared logic: they were a comfort to Donna. Things if not to live or die by, then to dream by instead.

But not one of them, not fucking one, seemed to have a taxi card sticking out of the top.

Her mobile, she realised, feeling like banging her head against the wall. She found a number on there and dialled it on the landline, because she didn't want them texting her back with spam. Managed to book a car to pick her up in five minutes.

As she moved away from the desk, she tripped over the root again. The outstretched leg of the swivel chair. She went sprawling. Nearly knocked herself out. Nearly needed an ambulance to come and collect her.

Which would have cut out the middle man, but perhaps wasn't advisable.

She used the bookcase, the shelves, to help pull her to her feet. Closing her eyes, shaking the dizziness out of her head, it almost felt as though they were helping. Actively reaching out to lend a hand. Many hands.

She gave them a long hard look.

They'd always been useful to her, even essential, that was for certain.

If it wasn't for them, she would have no idea how, among other things, she started out on this earth.

Well, not just for them.

For Donna, that was the one image, the one point of crossover, that those old Disney movies got absolutely spot on. The opening tableau of the King and Queen standing over the Princess, looking beatific, looking utterly blessed.

The perfect calm, immediately prior to the point of upheaval.

Before the curse, the spindle, the garden of thorns.

In memories of her birthing, Donna always saw her mother's bed in the Maternity Ward like that. After the mess and wailing of the delivery itself was over with, she liked to think of her mother sitting in bed, holding tiny Donna tightly in the flawless shield of her embrace, while her father stood there beside them, kissing the cheek of first one then the other.

The happiest possible moment on the happiest possible day.

Twenty-two years and forty-six weeks back from this one.

Donna thought that if, at such an early age, she'd had any hopes about her future, they would not have involved the way she is now. Careening down twelve flights of stairs because the bloody lift wasn't working.

The hope on her infant mind, she thought, would have been for anything but that.

For anything but any future, even.

Would have been for that tableau to stay unchanged forever.

But babies do not hope. Not right at the start.

They don't need to.

They are hope, in and of themselves.

They are the front cover, clean and smooth, marked only with a name. Everything else – the character flaws, the scrappy plots, the inevitable falling back on cliché – is way out beyond them.

At the start, before that front cover is turned, any book can be a masterpiece.

By the end, most are little but a well-intentioned mess.

She coughed and wheezed, had to stop on what she thought was the fifth floor landing. Lean against the wall. Aside from the other day, she never really did much running. And definitely didn't do any with a hangover, or on a couple hours' sleep. She felt like being sick.

When that messiness begins to show itself, and critics launch in with their unfavourable reviews, who has the book to lash out at, to bemoan, but those ultimately responsible for its failure: the authors.

The ones who first opened its pages to the possibility of ink, pushed it forwards, set it out on its passage from the first capital letter to the final full-stop.

Donna reached the ground floor, and nearly collapsed. Could barely keep going.

But then that bloody woman, the one with the wrist tattoo, the one with the pram, walked in through the front door. And Donna had to stay upright. Had to try and look normal. Hope the woman didn't remember the hoody or pants.

As they passed each other, the woman was actually looking down at her kid.

Though whether this was to avoid making eye-contact with her, Donna couldn't be sure.

She hated that she couldn't remember her mum doing anything like that.

She hated that the happiest times she'd had with her parents were ones she couldn't remember.

Hated even more so that she thought of it in such a way.

There must have been other good points, she knew. She couldn't have been that miserable as a nipper. Indeed, she didn't think she was.

Perhaps she'd just lived so extensively, and so well, through the minds of others that any fun she had of her own accord had paled in comparison. Not as properly plotted. Not as many good endings.

Perhaps as well, however, it had been easier to deal with all the disappointments in her life when she looked for and found them in the disappointments of others.

She had, after all, read hundreds of books in which a tyrannical maternal figure featured, and yet, these past few years, had never quite been able to face up to her own.

45

In the back of the taxi, Donna tried to see the journey as something other than it was.

She tried to see this cab as a horse-drawn carriage, all mahogany-dark and mysterious within. Gold leaf décor picked out by the light from two small glass lanterns. A faint scent of varnish and rose potpourri.

Not lingering hints of last night's sweat and beer and takeaway grease.

Not red light to indicate that the doors were secured.

She tried to think of the hospital they were heading towards as some other old castle. Or a fortress, perhaps. Not built by mad Bavarian hands, but not far off.

She tried to hear, to see the fanfare that a princess might receive upon arrival.

But each time she got close to forming and holding such a vision, the taxi would lurch to a halt, and her eyes would spring open to see traffic-light red.

About halfway there, the windows began to cloud and swim with heavy rain.

The cab driver turned around in his seat while they waited at one set of lights, wanting to make small-talk about it, but Donna wasn't listening.

She was watching it stream down and beat at the glass.

She was thinking: *Thank fuck I've got a hood.*

She pulled the hood up before climbing out of the horseless carriage, and stared up at the grey-purple brick of the building that was really more a prison than a fort.

She made her way across the car park towards it, half-waiting for coats to be laid down over puddles that, otherwise, there was no way to avoid.

They weren't, and she spent the first few minutes of her time in the hospital attempting to dry herself off in the foyer. Rainwater dripped from her clothes and her hands, not onto marble tiling but onto the rough mats designed for catching the dirt from visitors' soles.

It was only as she stood there, shaking off the rain, that she noticed her boots were still tatty with tin foil and tape.

Donna went to speak to Imelda at reception but was told she'd gone on break. Instead, it was a heavyset woman named Zoe who asked what she wanted.

It's about my mum, she said. I was told to come and get her.

Zoe had eyes like Transpennine train tunnels, lids painted the dark green of hills after rain.

Donna Crick, is it?

Creo – Crick-Oakley. Yes.

Hmm. She blinked, like a landslide. *You'd best try Cardiology.*

Sure enough, Donna found her in that department's waiting room, laid out across a couple of seats and a small coffee table, sleeping. She'd stacked up a few magazines to use as a pillow, and the dog-eared corner of the one on top trembled just a little as she snored.

46

D onna Crick-Oakley hadn't seen or spoken to Sammy since the start of the week.

That was three days ago.

She'd been staying with her mum. She'd gone back once to get some extra clothes, and a toothbrush, and a few books, but that was it. She'd forgotten her phone charger, and forgotten the signal was crap over there.

She couldn't really get any except for a few places in the dining room, and it was too cold at night to sit up and text.

She could sit there in the day, but she'd been busy with her mum.

They hadn't talked so much in years, Donna thought. Maybe ever.

The wine might have helped.

Her mother had started by asking her to come to the funeral, and then everything else had just kept spilling out.

Bob's family, his son, had wanted to get the funeral over and done with as soon as they could, so as he could go travelling. Could take his father's ashes to all the places that he'd never been *in life*, but always planned to visit.

At first, Donna's mother had asked for half of those ashes, but when Bob's son had declined, refused her point blank, she *didn't have the will to fight.*

They'd been going to get married, Donna's mother had said. Bob had wanted to meet Donna so that he could explain himself to her, get to know her, promise that he wouldn't do her mother any harm.

Donna's mother even thought that he'd been planning to pop the question to her over Sunday lunch.

She'd been singing 'Shout' the first time she saw him.

She'd been down at the local, making use of the monthly 'Curry and Karaoke Night' as part of a hen do for one of her colleagues. The room had been low-lit, besides the disco lights flashing red and yellow and blue and green behind the stage and above the bar. She'd been pretty pissed, she said, and so she'd really been letting rip with her singing.

She thought she'd nailed the opening *We-ee-ee-eell*, she said, smiling.

She said that was what had made Bob take notice.

It must have been, she said, because she had her eyes closed for most of the time she was singing, not needing to check the screen to know the words, and when she'd opened them at the end, he'd been standing at the foot of the small stage, reaching out to help her down.

As the disco lighting had moved across his face, she remembered, she'd thought that he looked handsome.

And rich, she'd thought.

Though it wouldn't have mattered, *and it's not like I'm going to see any of that now.*

They'd enjoyed a few drinks together, and when the hen party moved elsewhere, Donna's mother stuck around.

I don't need to tell you what happened next.

She didn't need to, but, drunk as she was, she had.

She told Donna that it was the best sex she'd had since before Donna was born, and, furthermore, that Bob was not a little man.

She told Donna that she'd known she needed to see him again, and often.

She told Donna: *In a lot of ways, I wish I'd met him before I ever came across your father.* He wouldn't have walked out on her, she could tell Donna that. He had been married before, but his first wife, the mother of his son, had passed away from cancer. Devoted, he'd stayed by her side until the end.

That's why she had stayed in the hospital so long herself, she said.

She'd known what was going on when he stopped half-way up the stairs because he was having trouble breathing and had a funny tingle in his left arm. She'd known that, healthy as he was – he'd been an amateur athlete once, and still went jogging two mornings a week   men of his age didn't fare well with heart attacks.

Her own father had died in the same way, and he'd been four years younger than Bob when it happened to him.

On both occasions she had stayed in the hospital a long time.

For her father because he was family, and because she loved him as a daughter should love her Dad, and because she didn't know what she'd do without him in her life.

For Bob because he'd been good to her, and good enough to his first wife not to leave her as she died, and because she, Donna's mother, had wanted to be good enough in turn.

Because, rather than running out on her and Donna, he had wanted to welcome them into his life and share with them all that was his.

If her own father hadn't died so young, she said, she might never have thrown herself at Donna's dad.

It was one of the stories that Donna had never been told, and, after the fighting had started, was one she'd never asked about. She hadn't wanted to know that things could begin well and then end up like this. The longer the fighting went on, Donna had wanted to believe that they'd always hated each other, and that having her had been an accident. Because that way she wasn't to blame for wrecking their love.

As Donna's mother had told it, though, it didn't sound like there'd ever been too much love there, even at the start.

They'd met while she was grieving the death of her father, and Donna's mother had said that, at the time, almost any man would have done. It helped that Donna's father had been kind to her, supportive. That he'd seemed intelligent – but not overly so – and told jokes that she mostly found funny. But all she had wanted him for, really, was to fill a hole in her life that, until recently, hadn't been there. To help meet her need to be part of a family again, and to have a man in her life who'd look out for her, when she wanted him to.

They'd married young, Donna already knew that. They hadn't really known what they were getting into, Donna's mother had said. She'd thought that he would be dependable, and she'd thought that he genuinely loved her. She'd even dared to think that she would love him more as time moved on, and that there was a chance that things could all work out.

But she hadn't known what love was – not that kind of love, anyway – not until she'd met Bob, in that bar, beneath those flashing disco lights.

She hadn't known what it was to need another person in such a way.

To feel absent in herself when that person wasn't around.

The day her husband, Donna's father, had finally left her, the last day of the series of hearings they'd been to in court, her face had been a mask of relief more than it was of pain.

Donna had been distraught, but not so much that she didn't notice that.

Not so much that she didn't notice how her mother was almost smiling when the judge awarded her all that money.

That almost-smile was one of the reasons Donna had seen so little of her mother, these past few years. Why she'd never been interested in meeting any of her mother's new men.

She hadn't even known what Robert Edward Cornish looked like, much less his full name, until she saw his picture at the front of Huddersfield Crematorium. A smaller version on the orders of service they handed out at the door. They were printed on fine white card, with gold trim round the portrait, and her mum took Donna's off her as soon as she sat down, slipped it into her handbag. As a keepsake, she said.

Donna hadn't wanted to sit up at the front, hadn't wanted to walk past all those people, but Bob's son had offered and her mum had insisted. *I need you*, she'd said.

She cried into a handkerchief, as quietly as she could, all through the service. Donna put an arm around her, tried not to look at the coffin at the front of the room, tried to pay attention to the readings. The eulogy that Bob's son gave, his voice cracking intermittently, made it sound as though Bob had been an absolute saint. A perfect gentlemen, at the very least.

In the car park outside, Donna told her mother it had been a lovely service, and that she was sorry she hadn't taken the opportunity to get to know him while she could.

Her mother threw her arms around Donna, held her for minutes, weeping mascara-black into the white of her blouse.

A while later, after he'd come across to make an awkward goodbye, they watched Bob's son drive away with the ashes.

There goes my Bob, her mother said.

I know he's bound for better places.

He told me all about them.

He was going to take me with him when he went.

47

A starfish, an angel, she stretches out on her bed.
Has to, after the cramp of the single in her mother's
spare room.

There's no impression on the sheets from the last time he
was here. Very little scent.

Four days ago now.

Five nights.

She'd put her phone on charge upon her return, and it
buzzed for a minute as the backlog came through. Eight unread
messages. A couple of missed calls.

Even now, the occasional rattle upon her bedside table, the
chirp of a cricket, the call of a bullfrog deep in the swamp.

She doesn't move.

Her head spins if she moves.

Her world doubles over.

Her world isn't a swamp.

It isn't a greenhouse, it's an entrance hall.

But it is fucking hot.

She's on top of the covers tonight, in her thinnest pyjamas,
and it feels like the sweat's steaming off her and rising as mist.
If she looks really hard, does her best to hold focus, she can see
it start to dance around the crystal chandelier.

As soon as she'd put her phone on charge and read all the messages, she opened a bottle and filled up a glass.

She'd had a good cry.
She didn't even know him.

She thought of his son.
She thought about aeroplanes.
Leeds Bradford Airport.
Doncaster Robin Hood.

Arms spanning out across bedsheets like wings.

Where is she tonight?

Where the bloody hell did he go?

She's far too hot. And too thirsty.
She needs a cold drink.

War-ter.

War-ter.

How did they get in here? The birds. She was sure she'd left the windows closed. She can't even get to the window in here. It's blocked. Sealed like a covenant.

It takes her a moment to sit. A few more to stand. Then fall back.
And repeat.
And repeat.
And then at last break the cycle.

It's so bloody hot in here and yet the marble is cold.

Kirk was perhaps right, though. It is a bit sticky.
Each step that she takes comes with its own goodbye kiss.

She stumbles, gropes out to grab something firm to survive.
She finds only the wash basket, which collapses down into itself
and doesn't spring back.

She crawls over to the bedside table, to where she thinks it
is, and after a couple of bad guesses grabs hold of her phone.
Uses it as a torch, blue-white like a wisp.

She follows it.

War-ter.

War-ter.

The words fill the room, raspy and dry.
She can't see any birds. It might just be her.

Her throat feels a bit like she's been swallowing sand.
If she gets any hotter, it might turn to glass.

She thinks about blowing it out like a bubble. Watching it
pass through the light of her torch and then pop.

At one point, she used to think bubbles were fairies.
Well, that they held fairies inside them.
But she can't quite remember where she got that idea. If she
were to go through all her stories, no doubt she'd find it in there.
She's even half-tempted to rummage around until she does so.
But she isn't up to the task right now.

And anyway, thinking it over, it might have just been her dad.

Maybe she used to pester him in the kitchen when it was his turn to wash up, and the bubbles went everywhere, and she tried hard to catch them but they all burst. And she saw the name on the green bottle that made the foam in the first place, and she asked why they called it the name that they did. *Fairy Liquid.* And that's what he told her.

And maybe she asked him what happened when the fairies got free.

She stands by the sink and it's still loaded with clutter. Three glasses, some cutlery, some coffee cups, and the oven tray she'd been intending to use for the pie.

Not quite recalling where she keeps the rest, she rescues and rinses one of the glasses that's there. Fills it and drains it three, four times. Fills it a fifth time, but then sets it aside.

Another bullfrog belch. More midnight crickets.

Hey, are you getting these? Please would you tell me if its something i've done xxx

As though he's all that matters. As if anything wrong with her would have to revolve around him.

As if she could explain to him, actually, what the fuck's going on.

Hey Sammy I'm sorry I'm still at my mum's and the signal is rubbish.

I don't know when I'll be back. Xx

It's not you it's me x

She leaves her phone on the worktop. She doesn't need the torch now.

There's a sliver of moonlight cutting through the curtains.
Enough to pick out the beanbag, one side of the shelves.

Enough to show hesitant tremors around them.

She should shudder, perhaps, but the truth is she's not scared.
She feels much cooler now. Calmer. The sweat's mostly dried.
Her head isn't spinning. At least, not so much.

She feels like she should read something. Seeing as she's up.
Not any more texts, just something she likes. Something she
loves.

The spines on the bookcase feel gnarly and remind her a
little of her old grandma's hands. Pulling out book after book,
the leaves rustle like breath. She takes in the smell of them, like
sawdust and soil.

This one now, heavy leather, she traces the title.
She knows it, she bought it, but she hasn't read it yet.
Donna drops to the beanbag, to the moonlight, and opens it.
A little too rashly: the first page has drawn blood.

She shakes her hand, sucks her finger, and lets the book fall.

There are answering sounds, as of things pushing outwards.

The breaking of covers.

The snapping of twigs.

48

*K*nock knock knock like a wolf at the door.

Or *chop chop chop* like a woodcutter's axe.

Donna's in the long grass, in her long dress, with her hands over her ears.

She hasn't seen Sammy for nearly a fortnight.

He's come to call on her four times, but she hasn't answered.

Each time, he has said to her: *I know that you're in there. Please, open the door.*

Each time, he has told her: *I'm sorry, I really am, for whatever I've done.*

As though it were an incantation.
A counter-spell.
A release.

But she's the one who knows magic, or did he forget?

Today he is shouting, or at least raising his voice, but she still hasn't answered.

In the past week, she's only left the forest once, carefully, when she knew he'd be working. She's gone to the supermarket at the other end of town, stocked up on olives and cheese and red wine.

There are seven empties beside her, her own little helpers.
Some of them.
She's not really sure where the others have got to.
These are from the past few days.

She's been wearing her princess dress now for five days, maybe six, and for five nights as well. She's been sleeping out here in the long grass, to avoid being too warm.

The sunlight barely even spears into this forest, with the curtains still shut, but she goes out to the balcony on occasion to see how the world is, to see if it's spread.

There were three thousand four hundred and seventy-two seeds to start with.

These became trees.

To work out how many roots, what do you multiply it by?
How many thousands does that make? How far can they reach?

It doesn't matter. All that really matters is that there are enough to surround her, to cover her, to keep everything out.

She feels close to them. These trees, the animals, the beasts that pass amongst them. The people who pass her, who caper and smile and fight and sing. They're all such good characters. They're all such good friends.
And even alone, in the dark, she never gets frightened. Those branches reach out and tangle and look crooked and grasping. But nothing's what it seems. It's all in how you look at it. If she

reaches out to hold them, then they hold her back. They give her high-fives as she passes. As evening approaches and it's time to relax, she lets them give her neck-rubs and comb the knots from her hair.

Keeping it beautiful, as it grows out so long.

Sammy said she was beautiful, but she bets he doesn't think so now. Or, at least, that he won't in the future. There's nothing unconditional, nowt that can't break.

Except love, Donna. You can never get enough of that, her grandma had said.

True.

And what Donna loves is these stories.
They've never left her. There's no way that they could.
Their numberless roots stretch deep through the centuries.
They aren't going anywhere.
And neither is she.

But the axe is getting louder.

The wolf more insistent.

I thought you were different.

She still doesn't answer.

I thought you were special.

She still doesn't stand.

I must have been wrong.

She doesn't even move.

Then silence again, not even birdsong.

Then the lift doors slide open, like a drawbridge going down.

Then they slide closed, grindingly as ever.

He was right about being wrong, but not how he thought.

49

D onna Creosote *is* different. She *is* special.
    She's a knight.
She's a princess.

She is always a princess, after she's done things like this.

Whenever she finds herself alone again, she is always a princess, because princesses in fairy tales are always alone, this kind of alone, right 'til the end. Until the happily ever after.

And she's starting to think, as she steps out on her balcony, that the reason she keeps ending up on her own is simply because she prefers it this way.

She just wants to be here, by herself, overlooking her kingdom.

What's wrong with that?

Is it too much to ask?

Ever since she was a child, ever since she was little Donna Crick-Oakley, she's always chosen books over spending time with real people. She's never quite fully been able to relax in their company, to be calm and accept that they want her around.

Perhaps she's just seen too much of what can happen to people when they get too close to each other. As they build up and govern their shared little realms.

It's surprising, indeed, what she can see from up here.

One of the reasons a princess stays so alone throughout most of the story, Donna thinks, is so that when she finally meets her prince and gets married they don't have time to find out all the things they hate about each other before the story ends.

Ignorance is bliss, as her grandma had said sometimes.

Ignorance is bliss, and *Yes, Donna, 's'gone.*

Was she blissful in those last few months, Donna wonders. When her mind was failing.
Or was it more than she could bear, that all her world had disappeared?

Perhaps Donna has just seen too much of what can happen to people, whether they get too close to others, or lose touch, or not.

It's surprising, incredible, what she can see from up here.

Standing out on this balcony.

Swaying on this balcony, with her hands on the rail.

White-knuckled.

With her dark green dress, and her coppery hair.

Overlooking her kingdom.

The river.

The ferry.

Where the traffic light devil is flickering red.

Acknowledgements

I'd like to thank my family: my mum and dad, for their tireless support and for keeping a roof over my head; my siblings for keeping my ego in check; and particularly my older brother, Adam, for being my crucial test reader.

Special mention should also be given to my friends (too many to name here!) who have both put me up and put up with me over the years, displaying extraordinary patience and generosity, not to mention encouragement, in the hopes that I might someday be able to buy them a meal for a change.

Of course, I must convey my everlasting gratitude to Kevin and Hetha and all at Bluemoose Books. In particular I'd like to thank my editors, Janet, Lin and Leonora, who all went above and beyond to help me turn my rough-edged manuscript into an actual novel.

Finally, my thanks to those whose works were in my mind most strongly when I started: Milan Kundera, David Markson, Terry Gilliam, and especially Miguel de Cervantes – without whom this book, along with countless others, could not have been written.